who hurt you

A SNARKY DARK ROMANCE

CRACKED NOT BROKEN
BOOK 1

CHELLE WOLFE

Hearth Publishing
H&P

introduction

Sometimes life gives you choices. Therapy or a unaliving spree. Therapy was way too expensive.

I didn't chose the life, the life was thrust at me. I guess this is me making lemonade from the rotting lemons handed to me.

Someone found me and instead of adding him to my list I've added him to my bed. OR rather he's added me to his - his list and his bed. And the scary thing is? I crave him like I crave my next victim.

You can't fix me and strangely my mystery guy isn't trying to. No, he's along for my rollercoaster and the verdicts out on why.

Vengeance has always been the game I won. But my luck is running out. I might have accidentally, not accidentally, unalived the wrong guy. He was still bad, but he might have been the son of the mob. Oops.

The good news? I have a stalker, and I think maybe I want to keep him.

Don't let anyone tell you, you're broken. Everyone's a little cracked.

acknowledgments

Thank you for your support on my first dark romance!

In a world that isn't right, we need escapes.

Thanks to my husband for the support to get this book done. Without him listening and also taking the kids I wouldn't have finished.

Thank you Firda Graphics for the the skull cover <3

And thank you readers! Thank you for giving me a chance and escaping into my world of darkness where the girl gets the guy and she gets her vengeance. No one deserves to be hurt more than those that hurt others. Or so Halle thinks.

Come join me on the journey in between the pages. Join my Newsletter!

https://www.subscribepage.com/chellewolfe

ONE

parks

IMAGINE my surprise when I walked in and Rainbow fucking Bright has a man all trussed up like a thanksgiving turkey.

It's fucking hot as hell and slightly confusing since I'm used to working solo and I'm used to succeeding. Fuck, it was confusing because this wasn't how I would fall. I sighed and tried to stay hidden, just watching her.

There's nothing like the last gurgle of a plea from their lips as you finish them off. Except, possibly watching her breasts bounce as she worked on whoever her current project was, that might be even better.

Rainbow wasn't quick about her work, though. At this point, I'd half expected to be watching every step as his blood ran a river on his pristine marble floor. She had an art form to her work, and this SOB deserved everything she could dish out.

She was a hard one to track, but damn if this wasn't worth it.

Maybe I'd stick around. It had been a while since I'd had any good entertainment. And the way her body peeked out under her ridiculous outfit? This was entertainment on a whole other level.

"Oh, Mr. Brooks." She took a rather large knife for such a short little thing and flashed it in front of the guy. The smile on her face faded.

"You know why you're here, don't you?" My cock twitched as I watched her cut a line down his cheek, a sliver of blood trailing the blade. Her voice was angelic, and I loved listening to it as she continued to talk. "Tell me. Did you make it good for those girls? Did you make them love every second of it?"

I watched in amusement as she ran the tip of the knife down his other cheek. Over his throat, but without cutting him this time. Just enough pressure to leave a droplet of blood at the end. She squatted and her tiny skirt left little to my imagination. Hell, the whole outfit left little to the imagination. What the fuck was she wearing? And why the fuck was I so hard? This fucking hard-on was going to make walking impossible.

"Mr. Brooks, when I drop the gag, I'm going to let you make a choice. Now, think about this answer long and hard. On a scale of Jane Austen to Edgar Allan Poe, how fucked up do you want your death to be?"

Fuck me, did I just come in my own pants? I had no idea who this chick was, not really. I'd only just found her and seen her less than a handful of times. But today? Today I was so close to finishing my own job and instead? I was fucking mesmerized.

Did I laugh or take notes? I was so methodical and quick. Her? She was a fucking artist. Nothing I could find about her prepared me for this, this fucking angel of death.

I'd had to dig to find her and right now? It was so fucking worth it and not for the reasons my uncle would appreciate.

I stepped out of the shadows of the hall. I had to meet her.

"Hey Rainbow Bright? How do I get on this naughty list?" I sheathed the knife I'd been holding back into my thigh holster.

Being unarmed? It was a gamble, but this could be a delicious game and I wanted to play.

A peek over her shoulder was all she gave me. Like she didn't have a fucking bit of self-preservation in her tiny little body.

Or maybe it was because to the average person, she was the more dangerous animal in the room. A thrill, almost as if I were the one doing the killing, chased along my spine as I watched her take the tip of the knife and dig it into the guy's neck. He screamed, and she shoved the gag back in.

"That is so fucking hot," I said. Damn, I liked that she was a knife gal.

I was hooked and watched her every move and the second her wrist flicked my way I was ready to play. The knife she threw at me was an easy catch with a beautiful bone handle.

Knives were so much more of a sport to use over a gun.

"Thank you, Rainbow. But I already have one." I kept the knife for a moment and nodded back at her work and held up the knife as we chatted.

"I like this technique. So much more personal don't you think?"

She stopped playing with her new toy and watched me.

"Rude." That was all she said for a few more seconds and then, "Who the hell are you?"

The guy squirmed and tried to say something, but it was muffled from the sock in his mouth.

"Shhh, Mr. Brooks. You can share my attention."

I tried to stifle my amusement as she petted him. She fucked patted his head like a dog. The appeal was nothing compared to when she stood up and put her hands on her hips.

Her little rainbow flouncy skirt thing bounced with the movement.

"I asked you a question. Who are you?" she asked again.

I looked her up and down and couldn't stop myself from licking my lips. That set her off, and she came at me. Controlled, no screaming, just ready to gut me.

I grabbed at her arm, keeping it in my control as I pulled her closer. She tucked nicely into me as I pressed her against me for a second too long, and fuck did I enjoy every moment.

I wanted this to last longer. So I decided to play dumb for a minute. She didn't have to know why I was here, not yet anyway, and maybe she didn't need to know until the second I killed her.

My cock throbbed. Why the hell did the word 'if' invade my mind? If I killed her?

"Calm yourself. I could ask you the same thing. Don't you think I'd be better suited to get rid of the trash here? I'm stronger. Quicker," I said, looking for what made her boil. Would a threat of losing this guy make her crazy? Could I push a button? God, please let me push her buttons.

Her eyes narrowed, and I flipped our position as I pressed her back against the couch and her pelvis pressed hard against my cock. She wasn't fighting me, or I didn't think she was.

"Is that a knife against my cock or are you just excited to see me?" I chuckled and she pressed it a little harder.

"A knife. And no. This one is mine. You can fuck the fuck right the fuck off. I checked him out from the library first. I get to kill him any way I want."

I took in the set of her mouth as she said the words.

"Such a dirty little mouth from someone so..." I looked her up and down. "For someone so bright and cheery."

I listened for her breathing to change, and I pressed my hand over her heart, trying to feel for the rhythm to betray her. Hell, I just wanted to believe this little beauty was affected by me like I was affected by her.

"Hmm. You seem to think this is your job and I'm something you get to touch, don't you asshole?" she said.

She pursed her lips, and I locked my thighs around the leg she had pressed between them. She shifted ever so conspicuously between my legs, and I knew what was coming far before she could actually carry it off.

"Now, now Rainbow. We don't knee other people in the balls."

She growled, and I pushed her hand away from my hard-on.

"And other people don't need to touch my breasts."

I chuckled. "Touché. I could tell you it was to monitor your heart beats, but well. Yeah. It was more for my benefit than yours."

She had some nice breasts. No wonder she was able to snag this asshole so easily.

She sighed and let me move her knifed hand to a safe distance.

"So, wait. Let's get back to my hit. So you're here for Marty Brooks, too? The sleazy shit that—"

I put a finger to her lips.

"Shh. Let's not talk about his crimes in front of him. It's so much nicer to hear them confess to it all. Right before you, well." I paused and now I was curious.

"You know what. I'd like to see your methods. We can talk about the mix up later. You have me fascinated. Well, you and this outfit. I'll let you go finish him. What was it on a scale of Jane to Edger? Please show me what that means."

That got her attention, and she smirked. Either she saw the earnestness in my eyes, or she was too far gone to care if I was a cop. This little princess would need protecting, I think.

In that fucking moment I had some dumb ideas. I was in the business of risk, and she was something worth risking for. Perhaps everything. I didn't believe in love, or perhaps it was that I hadn't believed in love. Because damn, I'd never met anyone like her before.

"Tell you what, Rainbow. I'll let you go and then maybe we can go get a drink? This prick's got a real nice bar downstairs."

I hitched my finger over my shoulder, and she smiled. Honest to goodness smiled. "Stunning." I said without being able to help it.

Her lips twisted into a sneer. "Fine. But stay out of my way."

I dropped her wrist and lifted my hands in surrender. Anything to make it clear I wasn't a risk. Because fuck me. What a way to go if she did stab me.

halle

I WAITED for my gut to tell me this guy was an asshole. I waited for it to tell me he was going to cross me in the next second or better yet, arrest me. Instead, I wasn't entirely sure what was happening.

At the end of the day, my heart skipped the closer I was to him. The asshole twisted my thoughts, and my body heated into a fiery ball of need as I felt his cock press into me. On any other day I'd have cut the thing off. But today?

Well, today I had my sights set on an asshole who had hurt innocent girls and taken one of their lives. I would never be able to unsee the news stories of her body. The news had to blur it out it was that bad, but I had other access to police databases. Maybe the police didn't need to know that.

Maybe, with this strange stalker in front of me I could almost be delayed. But really? Anger coursed through me as thick as my own blood. I struggled to feel anything, but the creep I was here for made me feel alive.

Until him.

Did I like this new feeling?

I shook my head and remembered why I was here.

My dear victim didn't have enough evidence against him and that was a problem for a jury. Money was a problem for a skeezy lawyer.

For me? I peeked around my strange visitor to the pretty little wrapped up package of a shell of a scumbag.

No. He wasn't getting off. He'd pay.

I looked at my party crasher one more time and smirked as he released my hand.

"Bold move. What makes you think I won't add you to my guest list?"

He shrugged.

"Call it a hunch or that adorable little twinkle in your eyes when you look at me."

Hmm. "You're really odd you know that? And confident."

He grabbed at his chest. "Odd? Damnit Rainbow. Why you gotta be mean and call me odd? Fucked up, sure. Been called that a million times. But odd? You popped that cherry. I think I'm in love with you."

I rolled my eyes and tried to stifle the grin. Never have I ever met a man, well most any person, that could make me smile. I take that back. No one had ever made me smile and been left alive to see it.

"You're so dumb. Whatever. Stand aside if you need to watch. Get in my way? Well, I'll show you my new Girl Scout knot tying tricks."

He glanced back at Mr. Brooks. "Those are some mighty fine knots. Maybe I let you try them out willingly?"

This did get a smile out of me. I couldn't stop. I wanted to hate myself, but something about this guy had me wanting to smile and not wanting to gut him like a pig. Could he tell?

"Now, demonstrate Yoda. I gotta know. What is Jane on this scale and what is Edgar? Oh, better yet can I help?"

I swallowed whatever was happening to me, because damn it. Help? Help me?

"To be fair, stalker. I'm beyond help."

He winked at me, and I felt my panties dampen. F me. He was hot. He was hot and offering to help like a giddy little boy? Damn. It almost had me wanting to see what he could do, but really? This prick was mine.

There wasn't a good reason for the second glance back as I turned back to Mr. Brooks. He was different, my stalker, he seemed to be well aware of what this guy had done, and it made me wonder if it mattered to him.

I itched to get back to my work though a small part of me wondered if Mr. Tall-Dark-and-Stalkery cared about this man's victims. I didn't want to think like that. Couldn't think that there was someone who got me.

I flipped the switch in my brain. The one that let me compartmentalize one side of my life from the other and went back to Mr. Brooks. The man that liked me for my tiny little skirt and pigtales and it was going to fuck him over in all the wrong ways.

I squatted in front of him, flashing my panties. The fear in his eyes as I smirked at my own little private joke was delicious and had me licking my lips.

"You know what day of the week it is?" I asked him.

His eyes bulged at the sight of the knife I ran along my inner thigh. I pulled the sock from his mouth.

"Well, do you?"

He whimpered.

"Monday?"

I clapped. "Yea, very good Mr. Brooks. I wore my Monday panties just for you." I turned off the cheeriness and glared. "You want to know why?"

He whimpered again.

"You do, I can tell. It's so I can always remember the day I avenged your crimes. Now. Answer me. What kind of death do you deserve?"

"You're a crazy ass bitch. You know that?"

I tilted my head thinking. "Yeah. That's probably true. But I don't really think that's Edgar Allan Poe worthy. You know, the kind of death where I cut out your heart straight from your chest and bury it beneath your floor? Maybe Jane though. A long, arduous death before you get to your very own happily ever after in hell?"

The guy next to me snorted, and I glared up at him.

"Whoops. Sorry," he said.

I cocked my head and then turned back to my guest of honor and leaned closer to his ear.

"To be honest, I like Jane so much better that you never would have gotten Edgar."

The pressure of the blade against the soft skin of my thighs was more for my uninvited guest than the douche-canoe in front of me.

"Any last words?" Maybe he was trying to talk because he struggled as I shoved the sock back in his mouth.

"That was rhetorical. I don't care. You understand how this works right? Bite down on the sock if it hurts? I mean leather would be better, but well. I'm not into that kind of thing."

With a kick of my heel-clad foot, I pushed him over and reached down his now soiled boxers. Predictable. I slit the cotton fabric down until he was exposed to me.

"My, my. It's so tiny." I flicked his tiny cock with the tip of my shoe. "That's good, though. Less room to take up in your freezer. Because yes, I leave all the pieces to be found."

The knife reflected the natural light as I held it high enough that he could see it as I swung down and hacked off his shit. Nothing filled me. There was no happiness or sadness as he screamed into the sock and his body twitched in its awkwardly tied position. My joy came from the knowledge that the girl was smiling down from heaven now, her soul surely released seeing this bastard suffering. That made me smile.

"Today is going to be a great day, isn't it?" I said, and I looked up at my audience.

He wasn't repulsed. That was clear.

I glared at him anyway.

"Why are you watching me?" I asked. A gagging sound had me looking back down at my current project.

"Shh darling. I'm trying to have a conversation." I petted the guy's face like anyone would do to comfort a crying child. He whimpered but seemed to finally pass out. Or maybe he was sleeping.

"Good boy. Now, you. Why are you here?"

I pointed the bloody knife at the guy who I was going to call stalker at least for the moment. I kind of liked him watching me, but he didn't need to know that.

My gaze took in every inch of him and damn. Absently, I ran the knife over the shirtless belly of the fat asshole that I wasn't quite done with, but I didn't want to turn away from the strange man looking at me. He licked his lips as I dug the knife in just deep enough that if my dear friend was awake, he might have screamed.

I pulled it away and shrugged.

"Sigh. All the good ones pass out. Guess we wait for him to wake up. So in the meantime, who are you?"

He smiled at me.

"Your future husband."

I glared. "Not funny. I'm not on the market."

The muscle of his cheek twitched. "Not on the market or not open to the idea?"

I tipped my head up. How did one say that they were incapable of love?

"Does it matter? I don't believe in love. So, I doubt I will be doing this whole fairy tale romance, love at first sight shit."

He took a step forward, and I threw the knife at him. He caught it and my damn pussy contracted at the sight.

Damn it. I was down another knife and crapsicle, he was hot and good with his hands.

"I can tell you aren't a romantic. It's alright. You'll be happy to know I'm a patient man."

My project moaned.

"Oh, good. He's awake. Would you like to do the honors?" I asked the guy, and I didn't know why. I didn't like to share, but here I was offering. Son of a biscuit. What was wrong with me?

The crazy that flashed in his eyes though, the darkness that swirled right over the blue that passed as normal, had my heart speeding up and parts of me waking up and oh good Lord.

"That's the kindest thing anyone has ever offered, but I don't want to take away any of your fun," he said.

My mouth gaped. "Are you trying to win brownie points with me? Trying to get on my good side? Because it's working."

He smiled, and it was an honest to goodness smile that I couldn't blame on gas or his face being naturally pretty. He just fucking smiled at me like I really was as kind as Mrs. Claus. Damn it. He was a pretty boy, and he was a gentleman to boot.

Fuck. I would never be a victim, never again. But with him? I'd consider playing a little less bitchy.

I WAS IN LOVE. That's it. I was done for. And fucked. So fucked.

All these years of swearing my life to bachelorhood and here I was questioning crossing my family for a woman. A woman that I was supposed to be taking care of. And not in the way I was fucking envisioning as we spoke.

So much wasted research down the drain, because she was fascinating. This world needed more of her. My cock needed more of her. I made one awful stalker it would seem, because I would not be using the information I had on her. Well, maybe some of it. I knew she liked knives, and I knew she liked control. One of which I loved and the other of which I wasn't giving up.

Fuck. I needed her, but from what I knew of her she needed this. It had taken so damn long to find her and here I was fucking it all up.

I could or should have been done a while ago, but I had my reasons. One of them was I dreamt of her and couldn't stop thinking of her and this moment. It was so much fucking better than my dreams. The family didn't seem to question anything yet. Hell, I'd never given them a reason to question me. Not until now.

My arms crossed over my chest as I looked at the middle-aged, now dick-less asshole who was no longer passed out. The judicial system was fucked, and it was so hot that she didn't like that. Hell, I didn't like it most of the time. Except when it came to my family. We skirted the legal system, but usually we did more good than harm. Not this guy though.

"So, Rainbow. What will you do next?" I asked her. I was practically coming in my pants the way she looked at me, no, it was the way she attacked him with no hesitation. The blade in my hand was getting fucking framed as a remembrance of our first meeting.

She shrugged, and my heart thudded so hard I wasn't sure it wouldn't jump out of my chest as she fucking narrated. She played along with me and the panic in his eyes said it was physiologically torturing him.

"Well first, I think I need to show him a little about the pain he caused those girls. Hmm. Where to start?"

She pushed him over again and the bastard rolled like a stuffed sausage.

"What do you think is the appropriate size for—"

My phone buzzed, and I cut her off. "We have company. Just finish him, we gotta go."

This was going to get ugly for her. The hairs on the back of my neck rose and my phone buzzed again with an alert from the bastard's security system. Well, a system that was no good to him anymore.

"What? No. He needs to pay."

I glared at her and flipped the blade she'd given to me.

"You can thank me later and we can find another toy soon enough."

She wrinkled her nose, and it was damn adorable. She was

too cute for this job, but then again, it's what had snagged this prick in the first place. She had her part in this world well figured out.

"I don't like to share," she said.

"Fuck me, Rainbow. Your little pout is so cute. That mouth is downright kissable. But, sorry to break it to you we have about thirty seconds to get the hell—"

A door creaked. I reached down and slit the fucker's throat. It was maddening to not stay and listen to the last gurgle of breath, but we needed to go. I reached over and hooked my arm behind her knees and grabbed her up, tossing her over my shoulder.

She squirmed for a second, but one killer to another, she knew not to scream because the devil you knew was always better than the one coming through any door. No one was ever coming to help.

Except me, and that was going to make one fucked up story someday.

"Sorry Rainbow, we gotta go."

I was going to regret this decision, probably.

I slid my hand up further on her thigh than needed, but it got her attention as I started to run opposite of where I knew the men, my men were coming.

"If you stab me, you know you're going to jail, so hang on and shut up," I gritted out as I took off towards an exterior door to the back. These weren't cops, and they weren't there to check on any petty crime. They were coming to see if a job had been done, or multiple jobs. They'd find one. But not the other. Strange, though. Why? Why right now? I didn't fucking care. I had several plans. If plan A didn't work, plan B or C always did.

Except, with her. This hadn't been the plan at all.

I carried her out a kitchen door that led to a back set of stairs that led to a tunnel that led to a toy room that led out into an alley. Fucking shady assholes with money. The research for this one was at least fun, and this bit of my research hadn't been wasted.

I breathed in air as I kept up an aggressive pace to get the fuck out of here. And fuck me. In person? The smell of her all angry and sweaty? And the way she talked to that guy? My pants were tight and my balls were fucking chaffing as I struggled to nearly run.

"Put me down," she said and gave a good thwap of her fist to my back.

I returned the favor with a firm slap to her ass that was no longer even pretending to be covered by the strange little skirt.

She squeaked and stopped hitting me.

I looked around and realized we were far enough away that they wouldn't be coming for us.

"As my lady commands."

Her feet hit the ground, and she tried to kick me. I caught her ankle in mid-air.

"Rainbow, I just saved your ass. So perhaps you should think of a better way to thank me?"

She scowled.

"Who was that, back there? No one was supposed to be home. Hell, he doesn't have a soul to rely on. Not anymore. Not after his crimes were splashed all over the news," she said.

It was my turn to scowl. The way she talked about him.

"Princess, you are a true hero to the public. I hope they know that." She was on the right side of my moral code and that was all that mattered to me. Good? Bad? It was all subjective these days.

"Anyway. They were the cleanup crew."

Her head tilted as if she was listening to the voices in there. Fuck, if were they all as cute as this one. I shook my head. It wasn't nice to assume.

"Why were they coming so early?"

I watched her repeatedly for any clues that should make me want to follow through with my original job, but my gut told me she was mine. Mine to protect.

"Alright. I lied. This wasn't the crew you use. You have a price on your head. Were you aware?"

The tip of her shoe dug into a crack in the pavement.

"It's the nature of the job," she said and kicked at a pebble.

"Well, you fucked up. You know that though, don't you?"

Her hands balled up at her sides and it was then I noticed the knife she held in her palm was cutting into the flesh. A line of red started to trickle over her delicate skin.

"Fucked up is rather harsh. I'd like to think of it as I took out the trash and let the scraps live to spread their delicious rot throughout the world."

I couldn't help myself, and I laughed.

"You have a way with words. Well, the scrap you left isn't alive anymore, sorry to say."

Her mouth pursed. "But he was innocent."

Her lips deepened in color as she relaxed them, and I found myself struggling to stay away. One step forward, and then I took a few steps towards her and reached for her bloody hand.

"He was more innocent than the shit stain that you so sweetly took care of. The problem is, Rainbow, the guy you did kill? His family didn't appreciate the sushi they received in the mail. You really should consider ordering dry ice next time."

I took another step forward, and I expected to see fear or panic. Hell, I expected her to back away. Instead, when her gaze met mine, there seemed to be a perfect storm in those eyes.

"So what, daddy? Are you going to punish me?"

I grimaced. "Daddy? I am not your father."

She smirked. "What, you don't want to be my Dom? Punish me for being a bad girl?"

I grabbed her wrist and pressed down hard on the artery to stop her bleeding.

"No, sweet Rainbow. I don't plan to be your Dom. I do, however, plan to punish you, but not for whatever you are being accused of. Rather, for not listening to me, and now? Cutting yourself. The only cuts on this beautiful body should be what I put on it."

The clank of the knife dropping from her hand was the only notice before I lost control and crushed my mouth to hers.

FOUR

halle

HIS LIPS CLAIMED mine and the little bird flitting in my mind, the one that squawked a warning whenever it sensed something bad, never spoke up. It didn't push me to kill him, nor did it cause me to want to stab him in self-defense. No. I liked this far too much.

My breath caught as his hands roamed over my back and under my skirt. The warm heat of his flesh against my ass cheeks sent a burning fuse of an ignited flame up my body. I wanted to gasp against his mouth at the new sensation, but I didn't want it to stop. I'd been numb for so long I couldn't even be sure what I felt was truly real, but it was amazing.

There was no controlling my hands. I wanted more of him, and I wanted him closer. So much closer. It was crazy, but every single move of his felt like he knew what I was thinking. The bulge in his pants pressed against me and even through the tule of the skirt layers, I felt him hard and clear.

I'd tried sex before and I'd never understood the hype. Maybe it was the fact I'd had to kill them to feel any pleasure at all. They hadn't been nice people, so in the end I realized the whole thing had been unhealthy to start.

But him? Who was this guy, and why did nothing scream a red flag? Well, none of my red flags.

He pushed against me, forcing me to walk backwards until my back hit a wall. The second his fingers feathered over my thigh and under the shear and damn near pointless panties, I didn't care much of what he did as long as he kept touching me.

And touch me he did. His fingers played at my clit, too skilled for me to think he was a reserved guy.

"Don't stop, more."

I was begging. What in the ever-loving multiverse was happening to me?

He did as I pleaded until moments later the world faded to nothing but a bright white static as its chorus. I could barely stand.

"Fuck, Rainbow. Your wet pussy feels so good. I need more."

More? Did I want to give more.

He reached between us, and I heard a zip.

I reached my own hand to find what he was doing and moaned at the feel of the silky-smooth skin of his freed cock.

"God, yes. More."

He didn't wait for anymore confirmation, and it wouldn't have mattered. His teeth nipped at my lip before he claimed my mouth again. His fingers dug into my ass cheeks, and he lifted me before I felt the shift of my panties again.

Heat pressed against my slick entrance. His thick, warm cock pressed against nearly unused muscles.

He didn't ease into me. I screamed out against his mouth, his kisses swallowing my surprise and my pain and the delicious need that swam inside me as he started to thrust into me, not waiting for my orgasm to stop or for my body to get used to him.

And fuck, I loved every second of it.

He slammed into me over and over and over. I bounced on his cock with every thrust and every time he filled me and pressed so deep inside me, I swear I could feel every single ridge and every single inch of him. My fingers dug into his shoulders as he quickened his pace.

I didn't know where it came from, but the next second I was coming for him again and yet even as I came, he still thrust into me once, twice more, and then I felt the heat of him spilling into me. His body constricted against me, and I felt the twitch of his release. The walls of my core still pulsed around him and still pulled at his cock buried inside me. I felt everything. Every last twitch of his cock. The fullness of his cock as my body stretched around him. I'd never felt like this. Actually, I'd never felt that I could remember.

What had he awakened inside me? And could he do it again?

I couldn't catch my breath for what felt like hours as he held me. My body bordered on pleasure and pain as I realized just how deep he was inside me even still.

It wasn't hours though and soon I caught my breath and came to my senses. The shock of everything hit me. I'd really felt all of that. The numbness inside me gone, or at least where his touch was concerned.

I had never in my life imagined that simply fucking someone could give me a high so similar to that of taking a life. For this one time anyway.

I wiggled my hips against his slowly softening cock and relished all the tenderness that came with it.

"Thanks. You can put me down now and I'll see you around."

I pushed against him again, using my hips to make room between the wall and me. I almost regretted it when I could slip my slick pussy from him. I moaned at the movement. I could feel his spend seeping between my legs.

Shit, when was the last time I felt so damn alive? Aside from killing the Scum of the Earth, anyway. The answer was easy. Never. Not that I could remember. I had never felt, not like this.

"What?" he asked as I tried to force my way down off of his gigantic frame.

"See you around. I gotta run home and change. Not everyone gets Rainbow, if you know what I mean."

I gave a little gesture to my body and wiggled trying to get my panties to do something and instead decided they were useless.

He finally put me down and eyed me as I bent over and grabbed for the knife I'd dropped earlier. Quickly, I shimmied out of them and smirked as I spied his lapel pocket.

"A little souvenir," I said as I slipped my panties into the pocket, and then I winked at him over my shoulder and skipped off.

I was in too good of a mood to let anything get me down. The night air had never smelled so fucking amazing. My bike was parked a few blocks away. Actually, closer to here than it was from the house.

Sometimes things just worked out. And then my skip faltered. I didn't like the way I ended things with Mr. Brooks. I didn't like the way stalker dude made the choice for me.

I didn't like that he didn't follow me, and the strange thought flitted through my mind. Did I care if he followed me? I think I might have cared, but I couldn't dwell on it. I couldn't dwell on the soreness between my legs or the euphoria of my body. Killing was nice, but this? I wasn't dwelling on it dammit.

With a deep breath I continued my way back to my motorcycle. Or rather one of my recent gifts from a victim. It was far too pretty to leave, so I took it as a killing gift. If women got pushing gifts for giving birth to the scum of the earth, I should get one for taking them out.

The night was still young. I'd get home and shower and be ready to check out another book, as I liked to think of each of my jobs. You didn't get to call a mercenary bar the library and not call all the gifts left for those that did business anything but books.

The closer I got to my bike I found myself thinking a little too much on the guy that got away and how he'd given that asshole too quick of a death. He deserved to suffer. All those victims and he didn't even serve jail time.

My chest started to squeeze tight and getting a deep breath proved impossible. My legs shook. Not now. Not now, was all I could think. The panic attacks. The blinding attacks that happened the second the adrenaline left, and the reality crept in. I took a deep breath and the scent of HIM wafted up from my clothing. The memory of every thrust made the walls of my pussy clench. The more I breathed in the scent that lingered on my clothing, the more the panic attack receded and the next thing I knew I was in front of my bike ready to go.

My new stalker was handy. Odd though. He knew I had a price on my head, and he showed up to my mark. My job. They were supposed to be anonymous. It was the code of the library. It was apparent he was from a whole different group and that meant I'd probably never see him, not without purpose.

I pulled the key for my bike from my bra and started it up. My phone was wedged between my sweaty breasts too. Maybe at some point I'd figure out where the hell else to store my shit when I dressed up in these stupid little costumes.

This was self-preservation really. I just got so tired of the look of fear each of my projects gave me whenever they realized I wasn't there to give them pleasure. No, not them. Myself? They did seem to enjoy the torture though, for a bit, when my ass was out, and my boobs were in their faces. Or perhaps that was my imagination. Still, I left intricate designs all over their skin and I got pleasure from that.

I sighed.

I wasn't able to do that today. It had been stolen from me. I clicked on my account icon and waited to see the balance. To be clear, I did this one almost pro bono, but the transfer was there. Should I be worried there was a price on my head now? Maybe, but my paycheck wasn't affected by the hiccups. Which was good. I enjoyed eating.

I pushed the helmet on over my pigtails and swore as the damn thing fought me. Safety first and all, but this hair style was dumb. I pulled the helmet off and yanked out rubber bands until my hair ran down my back.

Better. So much better. Now to get home and feed my Richard. He was going to get the big roaches tonight.

I sighed. My life was perfect. A lizard waited for me at home and expected nothing from me but bugs and salad.

Heat pooled between my legs as the stranger's face invaded my perfect picture.

Maybe having something expected of you wasn't so bad. Except, I didn't have much else to give. It was all better this way.

The drive back to my townhouse was short. I always enjoyed when my work didn't take me too far from home, but sometimes I had to travel. Not tonight. Tonight I was able to get into the bathtub and turn on Netflix all before the blood had dried on my shirt.

I'd burn these clothes later.

The wind whipped through my hair and less than ten

minutes later, my muscles enjoyed the caress of the hot water as I sank down into the sad bubbles the bath bomb was trying to make. It was doing a good enough job making the room smell like lavender. I took a long pull off the tub beer, or rather the beer that would be my friend while I was in the tub.

The phone propped up perfectly on the edge of the tub where I turned on a series that had a lot of men with accents and a lot of blood. I just wasn't in the mood for sappy happy. Give me a petty revenge killing and I was yours.

Leaning my head back I tried to drown out the invading thoughts.

That guy had killed a prick, but he hadn't deserved a quick death. On the flip side, my mystery guy might have kept me from jail or at least a really messy get away.

But still. It pissed me off.

His touch though? God, how could I ignore the way he felt? I studied a small bubble on top of the water, running my hand under it as I thought about him.

When had I ever not only orgasmed, but had someone be turned on by my work the same as I was?

I closed my eyes and smiled. Maybe it made up for the quick killing that went against everything I could believe in.

Maybe for once I could dream of something other than my fucked up past.

Maybe, for once I didn't mind feeling something.

***

I blinked awake at the vibrations of my phone and the chill of the water over my body.

The text was simple and basic. It came through that new books were available. It was never a surprise how fast new contracts were in. People were full of hate.

My beer was now full of water and useless and so was having a crush. With a quick pull of the plug, I hopped out of the bath determined to move on. I waited to feel the chill of the air and shiver, but I was just numb. Numb again and numb was better.

The towel ran over my skin and as I rubbed harder, I still felt nothing. Typical. Except as I moved, I realized that I did feel something, and it was the foreign sensation between my legs.

I still felt the small things, like now, my lip ached. I wasn't all here, I'd been biting it and hadn't noticed. Fuck. Without meaning to, I was reliving the moment in the alley and that would get me caught. I needed to be in my game, in the moment.

Should I be pissed off or happy?

Was it okay to feel? Maybe feeling this was okay. Damn. I was a bigger mess than I'd been in years.

I picked up the knife on the edge of the sink and ran the cold steel over my naked chest. Tracing my pulse that raced with every thought of the asshole who had taken one joy and replaced it with something new.

The thrill of the cold steel of my knife running over my skin was new. I wasn't numb to everything, apparently. Just most things. It was too confusing.

I shook my head and walked out of the bathroom to get ready for my next date. A date that always ended up as a one-night stand, and I was always the only one standing. That's the way I liked it.

The only thing I wanted in life was to feel the satisfaction of ridding this fucked up world of the fucked up humans that were so shitty even Satan hadn't come knocking on their fucking doors. No, he hadn't, but that's okay because I always did.

Tonight I would wear my black pants and black boots, but I was in a pretty freaking good mood, so I decided on a pink top.

Whoever I would be visiting tonight would get a magnificent view of my chest and maybe I would even throw them a little smile as I cut off their balls.

I strapped a few of my favorite blades between my pants and the boots and hid one in my bra. I didn't know who I would be checking out yet, but I wouldn't be going all out like I had for the earlier douche canoe. He'd been too easy, and sadly I was up for more of a challenge.

No. I was in the mood to make everything make sense again.

Slapping on a little makeup and running my fingers through my hair, I shrugged. He was a lucky bastard, whoever I was taking care of tonight. I knew my skills, and I knew what I brought to the table. Looks might be one of them, but that's just an unfair advantage for others in my line of work.

"Alright. This is as good as I get."

One cabinet after another and I realized my dinner option was a granola bar, maybe I should try harder. Maybe. For now, I grabbed my key and another burner phone. People like me kept phone places in business. Just doing my part for the economy.

It took seconds to get around my condo thanks to its tiny and industrial style. It had several easy ways to exit, but heavy steel doors made it hard to get in. I had a lizard sitter for those long business trips, but otherwise I had no need to entertain anything or anyone. I shouldn't be alive anyway and I liked it that way.

"Bye baby. Don't wait up," I said and shut the heavy metal door behind me.

A few blocks later, and I walked into the Library and headed straight for the stacks. The smell of beer wafted through the room of the rundown bar. There was always a steady clientele, although most were shady as shit.

"Hey sweetie, want to come back to my place?"

I grabbed the large meat hook of a hand and twisted.

"Fuck. Let go bitch."

I smiled and turned to him. "What? You call all your dates bitch? That doesn't seem very nice, does it?"

I twisted harder.

"Ah. Damn. Let go," he begged.

I shrugged. "What's the magic word big guy?"

"Fuck."

I twisted my mouth. "No. That's not it. Although that word is always so versatile, maybe I should consider it."

I caught his other hand as it swung towards my head and dug my nails into the exposed flesh.

"Is this any way to treat a lady?" I asked.

A bead of sweat fell down his forehead.

"Now. Let's try this again and don't try to hit me anymore."

He spit at me, but it was a sad show and landed on my boot.

"Fuck you bitch," he said.

Blowing out a breath, I stepped closer and yanked at his hand, twisting it to a horrible angle.

"Well, let's see. I'm pretty sure that I'm close to breaking this wrist and the other? Well, let's just say I could give a DNA test later and claim you attacked me." I batted my eyelashes. His eyes grew a little wider.

"So, are you going to go dig your own grave or are you planning to apologize?"

His Adams apple bobbed up and down before he finally spoke.

"Please, let me go."

I did as he asked, with a bit of hesitation, and then put some distance between us. I had things to do.

"See? Was that so hard? Now I suggest you stop calling women bitches. Stop objectifying them. Oh, and just assume most of us find you repulsive like Jabba the Hut. I'd fuck a Jawa before I'd glance your way. Now, in the terms of Star Wars, have I made myself clear?"

He nodded, and I felt satisfied.

"Great. I need to go check out some books." I walked off listening to him mumbling behind me. When I glanced over my shoulder, he shut up and I watched the bartender handing him his bill. Good. No one asked for names here. Those that weren't regulars who stumbled in like my gentleman suitor usually found themselves in rocky territory and rarely ever came back. Sometimes it was by force and the smart ones? It was the creepy vibe. Not that this place attracted anyone upstanding.

In the back of the bar, where shadows reached far better than any lights, were the stacks. Once upon a time this had been a proper library I guess, and I loved it for its nostalgia. The scent back here was from very real books.

My finger trailed over the spines of books long forgotten by most, and in between the real volumes were the special ones. The ones that we couldn't check out, reference only of course. I grabbed one flagged for me and took a quick glance at the information inside.

A cheating spouse no doubt. It just seemed to be what a woman usually wanted. Sometimes they just needed help with insurance fraud because men were usually worth more dead than alive. I rarely gave a shit, except in this case I still opted for a quick search on my phone.

You know things are bad when your mark appears on Google, and you don't even have to look at the dark bits of the internet. No, there he was. I supposed I could make time for a man like him.

Anything to keep myself busy. Anything to forget my own men problems or rather man problem. The shelf gave me something to lean against. I shouldn't have any problems.

It was time to forget.

Checking out my reading materials, I headed back out of the Library onto a busy urban street. The job gave me an hour to make a trek to the other side of the city. Busy week, I guess it paid off to hide in one of the saddest cities in the world.

Then again, where was anyone happy?

FIVE

parks

IT HAD BEEN over thirty minutes since she'd left the library and yes, I was throwing some serious stalker vibes. It was my job to know everything. I felt green all over again, like this was my first kill. And even though I'd told her I was patient, I'd fucking lied. I was calculated and could wait when needed, but when I wanted something I went for it.

Waiting for her felt like an eternity. I was stupid and risking everything, but I couldn't help it. She was like a damn drug, and I was an addict.

So, here I was. Waiting for her, because I'd just set up this whole fake date. Or was it a fake hit? Fuck me. I was a mess. Still, you didn't walk in and out of a place like the library with rainbow colored hair and not have someone confirm you indeed checked out books there. She was going to get herself killed someday and I wouldn't allow it.

I rubbed at the tension in my neck. The other issue with her is that you didn't piss off one of the biggest mobs in the city without losing your anonymity. I could find anything I wanted to, even if it took far longer than I'd expected. I found her intriguing the further I had to peel back the layers of the onion that seemed to be her life.

The crowds thinned with how late it was getting. I leaned against the darkened window of the exclusive restaurant, watching the minute hand go by on my watch. It was late. Unconventional hours for some, but normal for most of the city. I couldn't wait to see her in action one more time before making my final decision. Who was I kidding? I wanted to bury myself deep within her all over again and I wasn't sure I wanted to stop with that. So here I was. A hasty plan just to get her attention.

Too bad I didn't smoke because it would keep my hands from fidgeting. My drug seemed to be reliving every second of her body. How every thrust inside her felt fucking amazing around my cock. I was going out on a limb here that her other skills, no, all her skills were worth risking everything for.

More people passing, fewer and fewer stopping to notice anything around them. It's what I liked to call drunk and hurry-up home hour. Maybe I hadn't delivered Rainbow to my family, but this job should buy a little more time.

The guy owed my family some money and his wife wanted him dead. Typical. This wasn't a job that my sweet little Rainbow would normally take. Or so I guessed, but then it wasn't hard to dig up what other shady shit he was into.

I would do what I could to see her again and if I had to solicit business to make things happen? Yes, yes, I would.

My pants already felt a bit tighter, and I adjusted my stance. I checked my watch again. It was fine. She would come. I couldn't do my job if I couldn't get my head on straight.

She was so confident, so fucked in the head, and why? Why had she made the choices that landed her on my list?

My thoughts took a moment as I curled my nose to the acrid scent of burnt cigarette. That scent wasn't rare, but damn it if it wasn't triggering to see the bright orange of the burning butt hit the sidewalk.

"Hey, litter-bug pick it up," I said nonchalantly to the prick.

He paused and smirked and wrapped his arm around some box-blonde bimbo.

"Nah. I'm good. You can clean it up though Jeeves," he said.

I ran my tongue over my top teeth.

"Yeah. No. That doesn't work for me. We all work together to keep this city clean, or well, cleaner. I can't exactly get rid of the scum like you as easily as you can toss this," I said and kicked the glowing butt back at him.

"Ew. Gross," said the girl in his arms

This time it was my turn to smile. "Sweetheart, I'm guessing you've had far dirtier things in your mouth."

Her jaw dropped.

"Close that sweet little trap of yours, unless you're offering."

Her whole body seemed to stiffen and the douche next to her turned a pretty little shade of pissed.

"Fuck you, asshole. Don't you talk to my girl that way." He postured and tried to get in my face. I still stood several inches taller than him.

"Listen, I'm not in the mood. I have plans. If you have a wish to give yourself an early grave via cancer, go right ahead. Just pick up your trash and dispose of it."

The guy puffed his chest out and got closer.

"Listen here you fuck-nut, I don't have to do anything—"

I cut him off with a flick of my wrist and a crippling grip on his fist.

"I assume this fist was meant to pick up your trash, but as it somehow got lost and headed towards my face, let me help you."

With a flip of the tip of my boot, the butt was airborne. I

grabbed it, and in seconds the guy let out a long string of expletives.

"You fucking burned me you—" he screamed.

I shrugged.

"It looks to me like you grabbed it by the wrong end. Sucks you're so clumsy."

I could imagine the red, angry blister forming on the guy's hand. He'd have a fun mark tomorrow. I twisted the appendage until he squeaked in pain.

"Fuck, fuck. Stop. You're gonna break my arm."

I bent down where his head was now to meet his eyes. His face appeared more pale than I remembered and the air smelled of a fresh he-shit-himself perfume.

"Fuck. Fine. I got it. Let me go."

I smirked. "No more littering then?"

His head nodded so fast I wasn't sure he wasn't having a seizure.

"Yeah. Yeah. Got it."

For good measure, I took the now mostly extinguished cigarette and popped into his open mouth and leaned into his ear.

"This seems like a fitting spot for trash. Now be a good little boy and go home. And if you feel the need to call the cops? Well, be my guest. I'm sure you'll love this humiliation splashed all over the papers."

He didn't say anything else. When I let him go, he grabbed the girl and ran along the street.

I turned back to the restaurant where I had a small audience.

"He was having some stomach issues. I offered him help, but he said he just needed to get home to the bathroom."

The woman nodded and her husband, or possibly just another sugar-daddy, now ignored me as he walked into the restaurant. Whatever. They were all so busy with their own lives I doubt they noticed much. I doubt it would have mattered even if they had known the truth. Too self-involved. Most of them were. People were predictable and stupid.

Boredom set in and I was about to re-assume my place in the shadows when I saw the very woman I was looking for. She had on a wig and her outfit was much less colorful than earlier, but my heart would recognize her anywhere.

Instead of sliding back into the corner, I stepped out, grinning like some lovesick puppy.

"Rainbow, you made it."

She froze and glared. Her eyes looked over me and then around the exterior of the restaurant then the street. She got a little closer, something I couldn't decide was a good thing for me or a threat towards my manhood. No knife pointed at my family jewels though, so I went with a good thing.

"There is no way they are letting you in there, have you met you?"

I laughed.

"Oh sweetheart, I'm not here to eat. Unless you're on the menu."

Her eyes remained narrowed on me, but still no knife. At least not one that I saw. But fuck, her scent wafted up and my cock grew hard.

"You inspire my inner serial killer, you know that, Rainbow?" I asked.

I waited a few more seconds, breathing her in. Imagining her hips under my hands again and the tightness of her as I slammed into her. What would it be like to wake up to her?

I nearly choked on the air at that thought. Where the fuck had that come from?

"And you inspire my inner rage," she said, and it woke me the fuck up.

"Is that all princess?"

She let me get closer. I ran a soft touch over the skin of her arm up and then took my life into my own hands as I traced the neckline of her shirt.

"I think I liked the other outfit. So much more to see," I said.

She blinked up at me, and damn if the lilt of her little lips didn't inspire something dirty.

"What happened to rainbow? Not that I liked that nickname. I'm no princess, but that outfit? Eh, I burned it."

"Shame. Perhaps we can find something similar." She said nothing, so I continued. "I'll call you Rainbow if you like. But, let me be clear. Don't shortchange yourself. If hell has royalty, it's you princess."

We were already close to the wall, close enough to the small alley that ran the length of the building that it didn't take much for me to walk her back into a more private area. Late or not, I didn't need to risk any of my enemies catching me. Or worse, hers.

She checked the phone in her hand. Had she heard anything I'd said? I was pulling out all my moves, and it didn't seem to affect her at all.

"Well, as much as this banter has been a real mood setter, I have a job to do. And on this one, I'd like to choose to write the ending the way I want to. So if you'd excuse me."

She started to push past me, and I pinned her against the wall.

"I know why you're here. You know one side of the story, but I have the other. I thought maybe we'd enjoy a bite until the two of them are done?"

She gave me an inquisitive glance and the crazy in her eyes said I'd piqued her interest.

"So dinner? I pre-ordered. It should be ready in—" I paused and glanced at my watch again. "Right now. Come with me."

She let me grab her hand to pull her to the door to the kitchen.

"Where are you taking me? What the hell is happening?"

The horns of the city faded as we stepped into the pristine hallway of the restaurant, that clean as it was, still was dimly lit. The sounds of sizzling and the smells of steak filled the space, and somehow the only thing stirring was my hunger for her.

"I'm taking you to the kitchen, I have a special table set up for us," I said and pulled her into me. "We could start with dessert first though?"

She didn't run from me, and she didn't try to knee me in the balls. I was winning.

"Why should I trust you?"

Everything about her was so tempting. I trailed my fingers down her ear.

"You shouldn't. I'm a dangerous man. But, if you do, I can promise you I can give you everything you've ever craved."

The little vein that beat along her collarbone, the one that if you watched it just right, you could actually see every beat of your victim's heart, and it told me I was definitely affecting her. Just like she was affecting me.

"Tell me, what am I craving?" she asked.

Before we got to the kitchen, I paused and turned her to me. I pressed my mouth to hers and coaxed her lips to dance with mine.

I pulled my face away from hers.

"Me, princess. You're craving me."

halle

HIS LIPS TASTED SO DAMN good I forgot all about the smell of delicious food. I wanted him. I wanted whatever the fuck he was going to call dessert too. I grabbed his hand and pressed it against my breast.

Fuck. I craved his touch.

His lips pulled away from mine, but I wasn't done. My fingers wrapped into the fabric of his shirt and yanked him closer.

"Don't make me get violent, Romeo."

His lips pulled back into a smile, and my panties dampened. Oh, he was a pretty, pretty man. I knew there were corded muscles under this shirt, and I hadn't yet seen them. I'd felt him, but I had a new fantasy. No. I had a fantasy, period. Him.

"Oh princess, I'm begging you to get violent."

My breath hitched. My dark side, the one that pulled me day in and day out in order to keep the demons at bay was my mask. And it chased away more than just my past. People. People didn't like my dark side. But him?

"Ah, you like that don't you," he asked.

My lips wouldn't work. I was speechless.

"Let's get dinner. We don't want to keep our guests waiting. I suspect we have another half hour."

Right. We had work to do.

"Wait. Why are you here?"

My brain was slowly catching up to the fact that he was here, and I was supposed to be solo, and I worked anonymously. The assignments were tossed into books that went by call numbers specific to each reader, as I liked to call myself. A reader of people's sins.

"I told you. You pissed off some bad men. No surprise, I'm sure. But in the meantime, I'm playing judge and the jury is out on you. So tonight I thought we'd play and see where the evening takes us. And, with me? I can keep you close."

Close? What did that mean? This all seemed strange. Had I pissed off the wrong people? Probably. Had I expected them to retaliate? Maybe. Had I expected this?

Well, I didn't have a fucking crystal ball, so no. And seriously, I wouldn't have ever thought that being touched by anyone would ever be something I wanted. Ever. But something in the way he watched me, like he was just as cracked in the head as me, had my heart waking up from its little sleeping beauty slumber. It hadn't taken true love's kiss, just a little violence in the name of well, me.

"Play? So, is this just a game? Like you think you're the cat and I'm the mouse?"

I followed him without hesitation though, even if I had enough sense to question him. I also had the sick fascination to see where this could go. There was no stopping me from making this possibly epic mistake.

I licked my lips as he walked in front of me. I didn't stop to admire much outside of my work. This man, though?

"Enjoying the view, Rainbow?"

I looked up to see him watching me as if he didn't need to know where he was leading me.

"Just trying to decide how big of a hole I'll need to dig later." And I batted my eyes at him.

The sound of his deep and seductive laugh had me trying to cross my damn legs.

He rounded on me, wrapping me in his arms. He caged me and I wasn't fighting it. Not even a little.

"Sweetheart, the holes you'll be digging are the ones for those that try to harm you. "And," he said and leaned closer, "I'd like to think that this is more of a game of viper vs minx." He leaned in and licked at my throat. "Both will win, but no one's leaving without some damage."

I shivered at the excitement racing in my pulse.

"Who hurt you?" I asked with a smirk.

He shrugged and pulled away. This time I grabbed him and slammed my lips against his. He kissed me back and his hands gripped my ass just this side of pain. There would be bruises later, I was certain. I finally pulled away from him and he lowered my feet back to the floor.

"Cause, fuck I hope it's me. Now where's dinner?" I said.

There was a hint of a smile as I grabbed his hand and pulled him to the only opening off of the industrial hall.

A few seconds in silence and I found the delicious scents and the heat of a fire as it flamed high in a pan for all of a couple of seconds.

"Hey, Parks," said an older man. He wiped his hands on the apron and tapped at the other guy in a white coat next to him.

I looked up at my Romeo and eyed him. "Parks?" I mouthed.

He ignored me as he embraced the man in a hug.

"My table ready?"

They exchanged a few words that I couldn't hear well over the business of the kitchen, or maybe it was I didn't care. This was strange. This man hugged someone? He had someone other than me to hug. I eyed the older guy again and decided he seemed innocent enough. He seemed nice even. Why would he hug a freak like Parks? Did he know what he could do with his hands? I bit my lip as I remembered everything I knew he could do. I was so screwed. I needed to walk away.

I turned to get out of the kitchen and was stopped by his firm hand around my upper arm. My pulse tried to spike as I realized I needed out, that I needed to run. I was sure I could get away. But something in his touch had me stopping and my pulse questioning what we wanted to do. Why wasn't I running? Why? I didn't trust people. When I thought this guy was just a plaything it was all fine. But here? He was a fucking person. I didn't do people. Well, I mean, I did people. I didn't people though.

Shit. Shit. Shit.

"Wait there, Rainbow. Table's this way."

His grip was far too tight for him not to know what I was thinking.

"Hey Pops, this is..." and he paused. The way he looked at me, it felt like he was waiting for me to be okay with what the fuck ever this was.

I swallowed and then I did something that would earn Parks a few fucking scars if he ever hurt me. I gave him my name.

"Halle."

The slow parting of his lips to create a smile, I swear made him look human. Made him appear almost boy-like, and it did something to me I didn't want to admit. Fine. I admit it.

Here was one person on this entire planet that I didn't

fucking care what he'd done ever. No. I didn't care what he'd done or what he'd do as long as he fucking did it with me.

The panic subsided, for now. But the itch that I needed to scratch was starting to roar in its place.

"How much longer?" I asked.

parks

SOMETHING CRACKED inside my fucking heart at the sound of her name. My fucking soul had a heart attack at the idea that she'd just showed me her cards. Well, one of them. Fuck me.

And then, she'd tried to run.

"Ah. Halle. Beautiful just like its owner. Well, I'll bring out the food. This is my Parks table. Sit, enjoy."

I watched as he walked away, and then I reached for her, Halle.

"Parks is my name and now I know yours." I couldn't stop myself from shifting closer to her instead of the table. I half expected her to pull away, or better yet, stab me. But she did neither. So far, I wasn't entirely sure what I was truly doing other than trusting my gut. It was always right, and it screamed that she was mine the second I saw her. Strange to think that she was mine.

We seemed to be stuck in a staring contest. Who would make the first move. Would she run if I let go or not?

"We'll be ready soon. Swear."

She didn't say anything, but something seemed to shift in her energy. She placed her hand over mine.

"Okay," was all she said.

I loosened my fingers a bit, but still not too much, and repeated her.

"Okay."

There was something in the way she licked her lower lip that made her seem human. Well, more human than the gorgeous monster I was obsessed with.

"Okay."

And this time I released her, pulling out her chair while keeping my eyes on her. Not so much as a single muscle seemed to tense and under the tight clothes she wore, I'm sure I'd have noticed. Something that changed it all for me was when she stood on her tips toes to place the softest kiss on my lips instead of sitting down. It lasted all of a second and, well.

I wanted to keep her.

My phone buzzed, shifting my attention. I sighed against her lips but pulled away. It took a quick glance at the screen to see an alert.

"Perhaps we postpone dinner and take things outside?" I raised an eyebrow at her as if I was actually giving her an option. As if she would actually have a different answer. Like I would let her out of my sight.

She didn't turn all the way to me, but I could see the gleam in her eyes.

"Why are we delaying?"

I shrugged. "A little light reading might head our way."

I watched the wheels turn in her head. I tried to make this seem like her normal as much as I could. I didn't want to scare her off, not now. My manners probably matched more of the rogue killers, but that was who I was.

I liked that I kept her guessing. Women like her always had

the read on people. Always knew what they were walking into, she had to.

"I've never seen you at the library. Are you a librarian?" she asked, as I wrapped her arm around mine and we started to walk out into the general dining area.

I shrugged. "Once. But we all outgrow books from time to time. So, shall we?"

She shifted closer and something clicked behind those eyes. I could watch the darkness fall into place, and my cock grew even harder.

"You look hot as shit when you switch on."

She smirked, and it twisted her mouth to just this side of psycho.

"Hmm. And you? Well, let's see you work before I decide if I keep you or not."

The snake inside me coiled, waiting to strike. I could be what she wanted, but it wasn't just for the kill. No. This was for much more. I wanted to impress this beautiful creature of mine. I wanted to be her monster.

"Then let's go."

Her hand slid over my arm, and she fell into my stride. This close, it was apparent how much taller than her I was, and it was something that worked in my favor and not just for fucking her up against a wall. No. It made her seem small and unassuming. No one would suspect her when shit hit the fan, and it would. It always did.

We passed the girl at the front who smiled and waved. I nodded and felt a sharp point against my waist.

A tiny whisper tried to reach my ear.

"Hey, lover boy. You touch her? Is that why she helped you out? You're not that good at fucking-"

I cut her off as I quickly and yet ever so gently grabbed the blade from her hand and pulled her in close as we exited the door. In a single fluid motion I had her wrists wrapped in my hand and her leaned back, her breasts pressed into my chest.

My face was so close that her breath feathered over my lips, and I could taste the mint lingering there.

"Oh princess, you didn't seem to complain, did you?"

She smirked. "Yeah, but it wasn't slave making worthy."

Fuck me.

"You want me, I can hear it in your heartbeat. Tell me again how I didn't rock your world."

Any passerby, if there were any, would assume I was a loving partner kissing my mistress. But me?

"Tell you what, Rainbow. Let's go play a little, and then? I'll let you show me what it is to make you mine."

"Go fuck yourself," she said.

"Fuck. I need to get different pants if you keep talking to me like that." I had to adjust my cock because the amount of malice she could put into such soft words made me hard.

I hesitated as I watched her eyes dart over my face. Would she bite me if I kissed her?

"I'm going to kiss you now."

And I did, smashing my lips to hers and making this a kiss of promise or perhaps a kiss to prove to myself she was real.

I released her and the sound that escaped her mouth didn't do my already tight pants any favors. I didn't want to stop. Job or no job. Suddenly all the joy in the world meant nothing without her happy and by my side. I was in deep shit, and I couldn't tell you how.

I let her wrists go as I righted her.

"So?" she said and tried to pull her hand away.

"No, princess. I didn't sleep with her."

I handed her back the blade. I was still surprised and proud she'd been able to pull the thing on me.

"Rainbow, we need to catch up with someone, so maybe we talk about my exes later."

Both of us looked in the direction together and saw the shadows moving away.

She went from crazy to focused in all of one second. Confusing she was. Entertaining? That too. She started to skip ahead of me before chiding.

"And when we do talk about them, you get to go dig all the holes."

I laughed.

"You're insane."

She glanced back.

"You have no idea."

halle

PARKS DIDN'T NOTICE me glancing back at the girl standing at the door as I kissed him. Maybe he hadn't slept with her, but she sure as hell wanted to sleep with him.

I had questions. And most of them were for me.

Why would I trust anything he said? Probably because he hadn't lied to me. He told me who he was, took me somewhere where I saw him outside of his job.

I hated the idea that I loved the way his arm felt around my shoulders. I'd psychoanalyze myself later. It would have been a good idea to talk to my therapist about all of this. I stressed, would have been. Past tense. He met an early ending when he tried to use his position to come onto me.

Wonderful memories.

Deep breaths. I was doing my deep breathing. Because I needed to clear my head. Mad was easier. And I could get mad at Parks all over again. Why? Because. Because mad meant that I'd be able to make this all go my way. Emotions clouded judgment and judgment kept me straight and narrow. Or rather kept me killing the right people. I had morals, they just weren't what everyone else thought they should be.

"Shit," I said as I tripped over the uneven sidewalk. I was off my game.

"You always this graceful, Rainbow?"

The feel of his hands gripping my arm should have fueled my irritation and instead it just confused me. Everything about him confused me.

"I'm fine. Where are they? Did I fuck this up?"

I was yelling at myself to clear my head, and he smirked.

"I did the homework on this couple. They aren't going to get away."

It was hard to hide the fact his words made me bristle.

"What do you mean that you did your research on them? Once again. He was mine. How did you? Well, just how are you in two places that you shouldn't have been? I've never seen you at the library. Do you even have a card?"

He pulled me along and I followed, keeping my voice low. There were no answers coming my way, and it was driving me crazy. I might be off my game, and this might feel like a setup, but I also was curious and didn't care. I knew me and how and why I did the job. But him? In all my years figuring out how to have a reputation that people begged to hire, I'd never once been followed or found.

"Answer me. Aside from the Library, I'm just going to squash the fucking elephant in the room, or well, street. How are you finding me? This has never happened before."

He glanced in front of us and followed to where the couple still strolled. Strange that rich people would choose to walk anywhere.

"Why are they walking? Where's their car? In fact, nothing about this feels like it should," I said.

He let out something I'd call a growl and grabbed my arm and pulled me into a small alcove that maybe served a purpose circa nineteenth century. Now though? Well, it was dark.

"Shouldn't we have them here, in the dark, if you planned to revoke their library cards?"

He pressed his body against mine, the heat of his breath tickling against my cheek as he leaned further into me.

I gasped at the feel of his cock against my leg.

"How are you hard already? We haven't killed him yet." Dirty thoughts decided to race through my head instead of what I was supposed to be focused on.

I wanted to cross my legs and stop the throbbing that went along with the idea of not only murdering someone, but what Parks could do with that thing.

"You talk an awful lot. Has anyone ever told you that? Stop talking for five fucking minutes or you're going to ruin this. I will answer every question you have after." His voice was low and gravely.

I threw an elbow and the only thing that indicated I'd hit him was a small thud and the fact he grabbed for my wrists.

"What, you only have one move?" I said and had every intention of snickering. Instead though, he stole my words and my breath. The punishing kiss this time was hard and near painful and I guess that answered why he had a hard-on right now.

It took a lot of restraint on my part, however, because I wanted to bite him and close the door on whatever this was. He was in my head, and it was wrong. It was pissing me off, and it was making this harder and messier. I needed my head in the game. But damn. Why would I give this up?

I wanted to taste him. I wanted to taste him over and over and—he pulled away.

"You're an asshole."

I could imagine his brow wrinkle at that, but it was dark and all I could really see was the reflection of the streetlight in his eyes.

"And you don't shut up. Cute as you are. I've done my research on you. It took a while, that's why I've just now shown up. You're good at hiding. And this job is easy. Maybe I have my ways of making sure you couldn't turn down the offer."

My head started to spin a little. He was able to track me down? What the ever-loving fuck was happening and how could I control it? I needed control. I needed control, or I lost my mind.

"What are you talking about?"

He pressed my wrists over my head, and I didn't fight it. I didn't fight much.

"Do you listen? You pissed off the wrong people and I'm your grim reaper."

I shivered, and it had nothing to do with the night air.

"The grim reaper? Really. Then do it. End me."

The darkness heightened all my senses. One being that if someone knew who I was, then it was time for me to be okay with my own end. Sometimes it wasn't worth fighting the inevitable.

His breathing hitched though, and he didn't move so I rubbed my pelvis against him, intending to get this attention or distract, and instead I instantly regretted it.

"Tell you what." I tried to move to my tiptoes to reach his ear and settled for halfway there. "Fuck me and then kill me. I won't run," I said.

My hands moved as he pushed them together, and one hand gripped my wrists in his.

His free hand trailed over my arm, down my side, down to my stomach, and I closed my eyes praying that he would keep going.

His hand slid below my waistband, and I held my breath. God, please keep going.

It should have worried me that I was this desperate. But this wasn't my first brush with death and if it came with pleasure? I would take it.

"I haven't come to collect your life just yet, Rainbow."

He couldn't tell, or maybe he could, but my eyes flew open at his admission.

"What?"

His fingers pressed against my clit and slid between my folds. Fuck. The way his fingers slid right on in told me I was wet. I was betraying myself.

But fuck, if this was what death could feel like?

"Why wait?"

parks

THIS WAS NOT in my plan. Fuck, nothing since I met her was in the plan. I'd spent years getting to where I was. My family didn't trust just anyone, and I was their go to because I was fucking good at my job. What could I say. I love my job.

Blood might have been thicker than water, but it got you dead all the same if you fucked with the family.

But her? I suddenly wanted to play with fire and if I got burned? Fuck, I wouldn't get to that point.

"Princess, you're so wet for me," I said and pressed my fingers against her slick slit.

It didn't take much for me to find her sensitive nub. I ran my finger over it and loved the sound of her erratic breathing with each stroke. I pressed a little harder and was thanked with her nails digging into my arms. She moaned, and that just made me want to fucking play longer.

"I think I like the idea of fucking you and then fucking you again." I nipped at her ear and held my own breath. Both were so true. The idea that I could come home to this and wake up to her body seemed more and more appealing. What consequences would I suffer for taking what I wanted? Ones I was fucking willing to pay.

She quivered under my touch and my pulse reacted to her, loving her.

"Yes, much better warm and alive." I licked at her lips, and I loved how her teeth nipped at my tongue except I was faster, and she didn't get much of me.

I watched the color leach from her lip as she bit down on it in reaction to me removing my hand from her pants.

"We can talk later. Our window is closing, Rainbow. Do this and we'll both get rewarded."

The shift in her was lightening quick, and she stood up, brushing the back of her hand over the throbbing bulge beneath my own pants. The set of her eyes told me the torture was as much for her as it was for me. I grabbed her arm, and we darted across the street, ready to get this over so I could move on to dessert.

We walked in unison, already more in sink than the couple we stalked, and they'd been married long enough to hate each other.

"I get him, right?" her whisper split my attention from the hunt to her.

"Yes, what would you do to him?" This wasn't a fair question. I've watched her enough in the last week to know her style and know her skills. I'm sure she knew and I'm sure she'd ask more questions later, she wasn't dumb.

"Mm, so many things."

She wasn't all here, not right now. She was already living in the moment she got her hands on him. She had somehow fucked with my internal moral code, and I just can't seem to break away from her. No, instead I'm changing the rules and the game and here we are. Instead of me doing things easy and clean, well, I tapped my pocket to make sure my gift was there.

"Do you think he's a screamer?" she asked, but she continued to follow me, her hand still in mine.

I nodded.

"I'm sure of it." Did I tell her he'd had one run in with me a year ago? That he'd already had several warnings?

I pulled her closer to me, although the streetlights are dim here, there's still plenty of people to see us. "Pretend you like me, princess. Blend."

On the other side of the street I wrap my arm around her shoulders. Just a couple in love.

"Blend? Hmm, is this what a couple does?"

I sucked in air when her fingers pressed against my cock.

"Fuck princess, behave. We haven't even gotten to the good part of the night yet."

She stroked me through my pants, and I wondered what the good part was anymore.

"True. But it's like Christmas. Or well, I think it is. I've never much believed in the holiday."

I stilled her hand.

"Princess, if you don't stop, we may never get to your present."

My steps slowed as I tried to think of anything to get my damn self under control.

"Fine. Deal. But is she a fun bonus, the wife?" she asked.

Halle's face changed, and the muscles tighten as she looks at me.

"Why?"

Why indeed.

"Let's just say, I've got my job and you have yours. I thought this would be an ideal date."

She yanks me back.

"Job? She doesn't touch you though. Right? Tell me why

she's a bonus or I won't let you touch until I can watch you. Problem, right? Would that ruin your night?"

A growl escapes me before I can check my frustration. I didn't like being tested, but I understood what was happening. I'd been her stalker, and she'd never even suspected me.

"You really know how to push my buttons. Fine, she requested you to take out her husband. You already know why you'd go for him. I, however, do not appreciate her or the fact she knows of you."

I grabbed Halle's chin between my fingers. "So, Rainbow. You do yours and I'll do mine, then you do me."

I winked and left her mulling over what I had just said as I pushed her inside a door. Yeah. I was fucked; it was obvious.

"After you princess."

The building had a service entrance that I just happen to already have the key for.

She shut her mouth, and I watched as her hand shifted as she walked in front of me. Good. She was ready.

"My plan would have been much different, but fine," she said and stopped in front of the service elevator.

I shrugged. "Better doesn't always mean any less effective. I set up such a nice date. Tell me this isn't memorable."

We rode up in silence as she watched the numbers tick by.

"I just don't see why you would have an issue with her? So stupid. She has every reason to hate this guy. I mean, there are worse," she said. She kept her voice low as we walked together.

I stopped her in front of the door of the apartment

"Ladies first." I moved aside, and she dropped to her knees in front of the lock.

"Fuck me. I'd love to see you drop that fast before me," I said, only sort of kidding. I shifted my stance. I loved the way her sweet pink mouth struggled to hide her excitement.

"Maybe you should be the one dropping in front of me," she said and then got to work on the lock.

It was hot to see her work it open in seconds. This wasn't an overly secure building, but it wasn't cheap either. Still, if you were an asshole, you probably should be more careful.

"After you, Parks." The ways her lips smacked over my name hit something new inside me. It was cute and yet? Well, it matched her spicy attitude.

"Why thank you, madam. Oh, and here."

I handed her a syringe to which she looked at it and groaned.

"You really like to ruin the fun don't you."

I pecked her lips and started to turn the knob.

"No. That will just resolve the noise issues as you torture him."

I didn't want to think too much of it, but the sparkle in her eyes? Well fuck, it hit me right in the chest. Damn. I'd kill to see her happy.

Pressing my palm to the door, I gently pushed it open. She licked her lips as her eyes met mine and she stepped inside.

Somewhere in the apartment was a TV that was far too loud. She looked one way and I nodded, but I grabbed her arm before she could get too far.

I whispered one more thing to her and then we'd split. Now it was my turn to test her.

"She hit on me," and I nodded in the direction I thought I'd find the woman.

Her eyes grew wide, and the set of her mouth made me harder.

"Make it hurt," she said, and she silently moved in the opposite direction.

Fuck. I was in love.

halle

THE WATER RAN blood red down the sink. I always wondered what it would take to get that kind of red in a dress.

"You have fun, Rainbow?"

I smiled in the mirror at the reflection of Parks in the doorway.

"Yes. Thank you. I wasn't sure what to think at first, but the way he couldn't scream much and then, well. It was amazing. ·

He came up alongside me and smudged a drop of blood on my cheek.

"Oops."

I reached to wipe it away, but he stopped me.

"You need a shower," he said.

My breath caught in my chest as he ran his fingers over my collarbone.

"Join me?" he said, unbuttoning his shirt.

Every release of a button revealed hard muscles under tanned skin and every inch teased me.

"I've never seen muscles like that on a man with a beating heart."

His face lit up.

"Good, because I'd have to go kill every man that's ever touched you, especially if you thought of them in front of me."

He winked and slowly backed up to the shower to turn on the water.

"They have some expensive shit here, would you like to sample it?" he asked.

I felt ridiculous but giggled. I'd never felt this way. In fact, I'd never felt like anything. Try as I might, even locking down this side of myself still left my emotions missing normally.

I stepped towards him without thinking. He reached for the hem of my shirt and started to pull it over my head.

"Okay," I said. The demon inside my head normally wanted to fight me and make me run but she was hiding. Something about this, about him, made me feel beautiful.

My nipples grew hard as his fingers traced over the waist of my pants. He pulled at the cotton and pulled them down, grabbing my underwear at the same time.

"Although I can say your little rainbow skirt wasn't a turn on, I find this satisfying," he said.

Blood dried in little rivers over my arms, and I tried to hold them away from the shirt, but I couldn't stop myself at the feel of his soft lips over my skin. He kissed every inch on his way up.

Fuck. No I had never felt, not like this.

"Fuck me," I said. I meant it as surprise, not a command but I couldn't clarify any of that because his fingers slid over my skin and my mind scrambled.

"Lift your foot princess."

I lifted one foot then the next, and his hands slid over my calves and then back up my thighs. The flick of his hot tongue through my folds, over my clit, left me struggling to find something to grab for. I worried my hands in his hair, pulling him closer with every flick of his tongue.

He licked and sucked, and his fingers dug into my thigh as

he lifted one leg over his shoulder while his other hand gripped my ass, keeping me from falling over.

Fuck. My heart slammed away in my chest as a pleasure bloomed inside me.

"Oh, God. This is so much better," I said.

"Wait, tell me. Did she beg you?" I sucked in a breath as a shot of pleasure shorted my mind for a second. Between each heave of air I tried to ask more. "Next time. Let me. Watch." I couldn't finish my thought because just as quickly as I'd realized my heart was beating away in my chest, I sucked in air as a deep need coiled inside me, and the heat spreading within me grew hotter and hotter and the entire world fell away. My pussy ached. I sat at the edge of the orgasm and then he nipped at my clit as he thrust a finger inside me. It pushed me over the edge and the walls of my core pulsed around his finger and I shattered.

His tongue worked me harder and faster and he thrust another finger inside my tight entrance, and I couldn't control anything. Light exploded behind my eyelids and my pussy clenched down harder on his fingers and pulled against the digits. He flicked my clit once more before he pulled his fingers from inside me.

I whimpered at the movement.

"Now, princess. I will fuck you."

What? What was he? He pulled me against him as he stood up and claimed my lips. I could taste myself on him and it was nothing I'd have expected. I hadn't expected to be okay letting him take that kind of control of me, but fuck. Yes, please.

My senses still weren't with me, but lust seemed to know what it was doing, and I moved my hands over his pants. First his belt and then the pants and then... Oh, yes, please.

I hadn't appreciated this part of his enough. I hadn't let myself, and right now? I was letting myself enjoy the pleasure.

I was being selfish. I'd just killed a man and satisfied the desire in me to make this world a better place one shithead at a time. And now? It was my turn to make my world better. I ran a hand over his long, thick shaft and loved the way it felt in my hand as I stroked him.

Just like with my victim, I wanted to watch him as I played with him. I stared into his eyes and the power there, the crazy that mirrored mine. My pussy clenched again in need. I was far from satisfied.

"This might be my second favorite toy," I said and then I felt the cool steel of a blade against my thigh.

"I'd be jealous, if I didn't almost agree." The clatter of metal hit the floor multiple times, and I realized he was removing the knives on both of our bodies.

"Come here, princess."

He grabbed me up in his arms and I wrapped my legs around his waist. My new favorite obsession was kissing him, and I did until the tickle of water ran over my backside.

Was this what water could feel like? A moan escaped me, and it had little to do with him this time. Touching him made everything feel so alive.

"I want to make you moan like that for me," he said, and his teeth nipped at my collar bone.

"Yes. Make me moan for you."

And without any more warning he pressed me against the expensive tile and slammed his cock into me.

"That's right, take me princess."

And I did. His massive cock filled me. I couldn't stop every whimper and cry of pleasure he pulled from me. He slammed deep inside me over and over, stretching me for him again and again.

The slap of water between our bodies drowned out as he

pushed me higher and higher, and the pressure built inside me again. I couldn't catch my breath as he took me.

"Come for me princess," and as if his words were magic, he slammed into me once more and I did.

Everything inside me exploded, and I cried out, calling his name as he took me again and again and the walls of my core pulsed around him. I pulled from him, taking what I wanted even as he continued to push me again to the next orgasm and over its edge. My legs shook around him, and my nails dug into his shoulders.

I moaned as his pace grew frantic and harder and God, I wanted it. I wanted him to push me beyond the pleasure and he did, until I could barely remember how my lungs worked. Every shift of his body, every ridge of his cock, seemed to find a new level of pleasureful torture.

One more thrust of his cock and he pulsed and released inside me. I wanted to answer his release with my own and God knows my pussy did even if I could barely hold my own head up.

He stilled inside me and rested his forehead against mine.

"Does that answer your request, princess?"

I might have answered him or maybe I tried to nod. I couldn't do much of anything. He just laughed, and the sound echoed around us in the shower.

"Come, let me wash you Halle."

Something shook me to my core, and this was beyond the orgasm or the sex. The sound of my name on his lips. I liked my name on his lips. Until this moment, he was just some fun psycho that made this more fun.

"Say my name again?"

A hand slid over my side, up to my breast.

"Halle," he whispered.

I don't know why I'd ever given him my real name. The name that I hadn't heard since I was a child, but I had.

And on his lips, he unlocked something.

I wondered if he saw it in my eyes, because something seemed to change within him, and I wasn't sure what it all meant.

ELEVEN

parks

"TAKE THIS," I wrapped my jacket around her and then slowly led her towards the building. My building. There was no option in my mind. She would either come willingly or I would be kidnapping her.

Her pink streaked hair didn't match the photos I'd gathered earlier, so I doubted anyone would take notice of who was with me. Still, I still didn't like risking her. Fucking family issues. I'd never been an issue until I had something to hide. I'd never had anything I wanted to protect.

She took the jacket without question, and as we walked through the doors, she followed my lead.

She wasn't fighting this, and I couldn't decide if I liked it or not. Certainly, it was easier than having to carry her in here.

I should have talked more on the way here. Maybe she should have talked more. Maybe either of us shouldn't be so damn awkward. My cock had been buried inside her less than an hour ago and yet, we had nothing to say. Or maybe we didn't need to say anything?

"Turn your face that way."

I pointed, and she noticed the camera without looking

directly up, doing as I asked. She was smart, or at least smart at not getting caught. This probably all made sense to her. Strange how freeing it could be to have someone understand your creepy ass behavior. Not that I really thought of myself as creepy.

"This isn't my apartment," she said to the wall rather than at me. As we left the vestibule, I grabbed her and spun her to my other side.

I was certain, even with her keeping her head down, she could still gather just how nice this place was. It was grand and gaudy if you asked me, but no one had. This wasn't my first choice of living, but sometimes you just did as you were told. In this family, you did as you were told.

"No. It isn't yours."

I pulled her along, which felt strange. Women fell at my feet, I never had to drag one.

"Okay. My curiosity is piqued. But what about the last place? We didn't stay and clean."

Shit. She was right. I grabbed my phone and sent a text.

"Handled. Now, could you please move your damn feet?"

I waited for her to resist. I readied myself for a fight, but she just kept walking, and maybe added a little speed to her steps.

I wanted to hurry her out of the public eye. Out of the eyes in this place. Maybe I should have gone back to her place, but the security there was awful. Her apartment was done up well enough, but the building itself? Well, I had added cameras and not one had been found or checked. Which yes, that was the point. But the more I watched her, the more it pissed me off she never noticed.

Here, I knew we were all watched. I knew that and so did they. They wouldn't expect someone they saw as a threat to enter, not willingly. But this was home, and it was a safe space. This wasn't where one brought work.

"The elevator there, that goes to my floor."

She turned to me.

"Your apartment?"

I nodded and slid a small fob over the plate to call the elevator for my section of the building. I grabbed her close, keeping the back of her head towards yet another camera.

"Just pretend you like me," I said.

She laughed. "Like is a strong word, Parks. But sure. Fine. Should I pretend to be one of your whores?"

I rolled my eyes.

"There are no whores. You know as well as I do, we don't have a fuck load of time or flexibility to have much of anything."

She got closer, her hands wrapping in my lapels.

"I have a dragon, and I'll need to text my sitter if I can't get back to him."

A dragon? I started to laugh. "That's not a real pet, princess."

She looked up at me as the doors opened and she yanked me inside.

"Where are the cameras here?" she whispered.

I tapped on her right hand and did a head bob behind her.

I wasn't sure why she didn't ask questions, or maybe again she was much smarter than even I'd given her credit for, and I gave her a lot of credit.

She stood on her tiptoes and still couldn't reach my mouth, so I met her halfway. I was a goner. When had I ever met anyone halfway willingly? No questions. No strings attached. Just did it.

"My dragon is very real, why are you jealous he might be bigger than yours?"

She pressed her lips to mine, and I could feel the parting of her lips into what I suspected would be something like a teasing little smirk. Her hand slid down the front of my shirt and over my waist band where she cupped my balls.

"I promise you that he is indeed bigger, but that's only if you include his tail."

I couldn't decide if I should moan and grind against her hand or grab her and toss her over my shoulder where I could spank her sweet little ass.

The elevator dinged, and the doors opened to my apartment. No more cameras from here on out. I pushed her backwards into the apartment and the doors shut behind me.

She pushed me away hard, and I nearly fell backwards.

"Alright, where are we and why do you look like you're related to Daddy Warbucks?"

I kicked off my shoes and pulled my tie out from my pocket, tossing it on the entrance table as I walked in.

"Because I am related to someone like Daddy Warbucks, only it's my uncle and his name is James Rossi. My father is Aaron Rossi."

I waited for the connection to work its way through her mind.

"Uh, huh? Okay. And I killed a Rossi, didn't I? So hard to keep up on all the names."

I unbuttoned my shirt and approached her. She backed away into the small kitchen until her ass hit the counter.

"Yes, yes you did. Very good princess. And what do you think that did to the Rossi family?"

She shrugged. "Got rid of one more asshole in the world? He wanted me to kill someone who had borrowed money. Like really? Money? I didn't have time for that. So I traced the buyer, which you know I shouldn't have done. But I found him and at the end of my rainbow was him. Did you know he got off on five," she stopped and held up her hand. "Five counts of rape?"

I dragged my teeth over my bottom lip.

"Yeah. You don't say."

I stared at her straight in the eyes.

"And countless murders and near murders. My life is easier without him. But before you acted, you didn't think to check that he wasn't part of one of the largest crime families in the city first?"

She didn't look away, and to her credit, she didn't run. She didn't even try to wiggle out from under me because at this point I was pressed up against her, begging for my next taste.

"No. I didn't care. He was guilty. He was also one of my earlier kills. I learned a lot since him. And look at me now. I mean it took you years to find me, so it wasn't exactly a huge risk for me, was it? And I mean, we gotta go sometime."

Her hands ran down my exposed abs.

"And what a way to go," she said.

The corner of my mouth quirked. Damn it all to hell.

"Princess, you're in a shitload of trouble and I don't know what to do about it right now. So you asked me why here? Because I know I can keep your ass safe here. The bonus is that I can keep your ass in my bed, too."

Her nipple was taut through the shirt she wore and begged for me to grab it.

"Yes, in your bed," she said and arched into my hand. "Under your body. Show me just how much trouble I'm in."

Her hand was down my pants before I could say yes or no.

"I think I'm in more trouble than you are," I said on a hiss.

My beautiful dark princess squeezed my cock and slid her fingers over the tip of it.

"You're mine, Halle. You understand that? Mine." And I kissed her, taking her to my bed to punish myself just as much as her.

halle

"I'LL BE BACK in a few hours," Parks said, nipping at my shoulder.

"Are you bringing back my stuff? I need my Richard."

He paused and glared at me. I was tummy down, naked in his sheets, while he was dressed in a very pristine suit.

"Richard? Please tell me you named your vibrator, and I don't have to go kill someone."

"You are so silly," I said, letting him get an eyeful of my ass. The laughter that followed was real, and it felt so weird to really enjoy someone's company. Or to even think it to be adorable how jealous he was.

"No. A Richard is my pet dragon. If I'm going to be a kept woman, at least bring me my friend."

He pinched the bridge of his nose.

"Right. Okay. Fine. Kept woman though?"

I watched him, and I don't think he liked the term.

"Well, here I am in your bed, naked. I mean, it's not so bad. Will you get me my own apartment and pay for everything as long as I fuck you?" I moaned against the softness of the sheets. Yeah, this wasn't so bad.

"But let's be honest. Men like you? You have needs and once those are taken care of? Well, let's assume I'll either be six feet down or you'll pay me off. Being that I seem to be on your uncle's shit list? I'd guess you already have a plot picked out for me."

I yawned and rolled over and enjoyed the slip of the sheet. My breasts were exposed. This was a game I could play. Use what I had to catch them. Right now, I debated if I was trying to keep myself alive or chase the one thing that made this life something other than numb, blind revenge.

He hadn't said anything yet, but he was studying me, and I was studying him. I didn't know what it truly meant that I couldn't walk away, and I couldn't stand the idea of someone looking at him, let alone licking him.

"It's fine, really. I'm good either way. Feel free to fuck me to death though, because I'll make this super easy. If you choose to pay me off? Sadly, I'm territorial, I'm realizing. I would probably have to kill anyone else you ever thought of dating."

He took a step closer to the bed. "You are a complication. One I haven't entirely figured out what to do with yet."

I ran my finger over my naked chest and circled my own nipple. I couldn't stop the way my body reacted to his gaze.

"Complication? Or a really pleasant distraction?"

I'd never felt like this before. Alive? Partially. But it was something else and I couldn't figure out what that was. Confusion didn't stop me from knowing what being in the minute meant or what I needed.

I ran my hand over my breasts and watched as my nipples responded to my touch with the cooler air.

"You do look rather nice in a suit, but I think I prefer you naked."

He shifted, and his massive length was easily seen as an outline behind those fancy pants.

"Are you sure you can't stay with me?" I squeezed my breasts with both hands and this time it was more for my benefit than his. I wanted him all over again.

Or was it that the itch to leave was getting to me and the only thing keeping me from running was focusing on the desire? So many questions, and lucky for him the sexy tone of his voice brought me back to this moment.

"Shit, Rainbow. I've got to deal with some business. Don't do anything stupid while I'm gone. The top of that list? You leaving and getting caught before I figure out how to handle you."

What was a girl to do when you were sort of being held captive by someone who had to have been the God of sex in a previous life?

"What makes you think I will stay here like a good little girl?"

His hand ran through his hair making the perfect strands go astray.

"Honestly? Not a goddamn thing. I'd love to say that nothing in this world scared me, but you leaving? That might, and I stress might, give me a reason to second guess leaving. I'm not kidding. Just stay put. I'll bring the dick and some clothes as well."

I stretched.

"It's the Richard. And fine. He needs his bugs too. Where am I going dressed like this, anyway? I assume you got rid of the clothes I had last night?"

The serious set of his features told me nothing except he wasn't in a joking mood.

"Yes, they are disposed of. Sorry. That burner? Also gone. So you have no clothes and no phone. Your underwear and knives? On the table. You had some cash too. I put that with the rest."

"I'm surprised you found everything."

No matter where this went, or where I went, the last day would be burned into my mind.

I was still broken as hell, but I loved that this part wasn't.

"Thanks for fixing my vagina."

I rolled over, and the sheets slid off my ass.

I watched him from the plushy pillow.

He snorted. "Was it broken, princess?"

I pulled the pillow closer and closed my eyes.

"Everything was broken."

A moan escaped my lungs as the heat of his hand slid over ass cheek. Biting down on the pillow, I stifled any more noises as the heat of his breath over the skin spiked my blood pressure.

He nipped at my ass, and I could feel the smile touching his lips with every kiss, and the line of tingling nerves down following his hand.

My entire body burned anew for his touch. My pussy clenched as his hands grabbed my thigh and pushed it wider giving him access. His fingers slid down until he found my core.

"Already so wet for me?"

I didn't answer; he wasn't asking. He was telling me what I already knew.

"Looks like your cunt works just fine to me."

My nails dug into the pillow. I swallowed a squeal when he licked my entrance and then slid a single finger inside me.

I couldn't stop myself and I pushed against him. He slowly slid in and out of me even as I felt the shift of the bed and his face came even with mine.

"I'll be back soon, princess. Be a good girl and I'll finish what I've started when I get home."

He kissed the tip of my nose, and his fingers left me.

"Mm. I love the taste of you. Guess that will have to get me by until I can come back."

He got up, and I heard the sound of his shoes over the tile floor.

"Room service is by the phone. Lift the receiver and it goes straight to the security. They have been instructed to leave my guest alone unless she needs something."

The door opened.

"Oh, and Rainbow? Be a good girl. I fucking mean it."

I giggled and threw the pillow, knowing it wouldn't even get outside the bedroom. Still, he chuckled, and the door closed behind him. His footsteps grew quieter, and I assumed he was in the elevator and gone.

I sank back into the bed that smelled of Parks and sex.

For this exact moment? This was enough.

I didn't feel dead inside, not right now anyway.

No. But as I lay there, I realized that I had no way to find out if there was anyone new to checkout.

Evil didn't sleep and neither could I.

I sat up and scratched at my skin as the familiar itch started.

No, I couldn't just sit here and wait. I would not be a minute too late to save someone else by getting rid of the bad people.

***

As it turns out you can only pace a penthouse so many times before you're ready to stab yourself in the eye. I wanted to crawl out of my own skin. If I wasn't careful, I would leave welts on my own skin as I scratched at the invisible itch, but that wasn't going to leave scars. Or maybe that's what I needed?

I shook my head and ran my fingers over the lines of scars over my arms. They reminded me of everything I'd come from and what I finally found that fixed me.

And yet I was here. Locked away like some damsel that needed saving.

I grabbed my knives and found a sharpening stone in the kitchen which passed a little more time. I tested one on my thigh, just a little nick. The pain was delicious and the only pleasure I would be getting while stuck here alone.

I walked back to the windows that lined the place. I didn't think anyone could see inside, not the way they were tinted, and even if they could, it was Parks' fault if someone saw me naked. The cityscape bored me though. There was nothing to see. Just a bunch of people that went about peopling, thinking nothing bad will ever happen to them.

Maybe that was right. Maybe I'd just been unlucky.

Well, I'd changed my luck. And sitting here wasn't in line with my dream board. The dream of unaliving at least one douche-canoe a day for 30 days straight. I figured the two yesterday might make up for it if today didn't go as planned.

I cleaned out my nails with the tip of my trusty little knife, thinking.

I was trying to be a whole new me. They said it took three weeks to create a new habit.

It was settled. I hopped up from the chair that had been comfortable for all of five minutes until I couldn't sit anymore, and headed for his closest. His closet was literally bigger than my apartment. Rows and rows of suits and button-down shirts. Hmm. I could work with that.

I grabbed a shirt and was happy to find that it was a lot bigger than me. I was average in all the ways, but he was a big guy, something I only noticed when he was lifting me and shoving his cock inside me.

My stomach flipped, and I rolled my eyes. I could not be one of those sappy girls who laid around just waiting for her next release.

Or maybe I could. But only after I killed someone.

I grabbed a belt and fastened it around the shirt. There. It looked just like a dress. Or something. I didn't really care. It was long enough.

Back in the living room, I started putting on all my blades, finding it harder to conceal them with my lack of pants. The boots helped, and they were clean thanks to Parks. He'd insisted on helping me clean up. Of course he had been perfectly clean, and I wondered how he killed her.

I sat on the floor and daydreamed about it. I didn't kill many women, only the ones who asked for it. That woman didn't have a good vibe, but I craved and thrived on info. I felt the strangest jab at the memory of Parks telling me she'd hit on him. Yeah. She deserved it and he understood that. One point for Parks and 0 for dead lady.

A ding sounded somewhere in the apartment. No. It was the elevator. I walked towards the small hallway and hit a button on the outside that was blinking. I mean what's the worst that could happen? Someone wanted to kill me?

But as the doors opened inside, there was a guy with a tray.

"Miss, this was requested to be delivered. Would you like me to bring it in?"

I glared.

"Yes?" he asked, and he pushed the cart forward, anyway. "Mr. Rossi will kill me if you say no, so. Uh. Here you go. Please let me know if you need anything else."

I grabbed at the door, stopping it from shutting.

"I didn't order anything though."

He nodded. "Mr. Rossi texted me to make sure you got this."

It wasn't lost on me how he wouldn't make eye contact.

"Look at me. Are you afraid of me?"

He didn't say anything and still kept looking down. Son of a bitch. What kind of man was I dealing with?

"Sorry, miss." He pointed behind me. "The sandwich is

under there and the box is a gift Mr. Rossi had sent over. Have a good day."

I stared at the box that he'd said was a gift and before I could turn around, the doors closed. I stomped my foot.

I growled into the empty space. Fuck me. This was impossible. I couldn't just sit here. I eyed the cart again.

A gift?

No one had ever given me a gift.

"I—"

But there was no one to talk to but myself.

"A gift?" I repeated to myself.

The little cart moved easily over the tile, and I stopped in the kitchen. I was lost in thought. Gift?

I lifted the lid off the tray and ate the sandwich, watching the box. It wasn't logical to think it would jump off the tray or that it would explode. Not if it was from Parks. Or had he decided that killing me would fix everything? I watched it some more.

What was it going to do? Jump? Maybe.

I popped the last bite of food into my mouth realizing I hadn't tasted it at all. It probably was good though.

Finally, I mustered the confidence to open the box.

It wasn't huge, maybe a shirt size. Tissue paper lined the box and made it look pretty, like I was actually some girl he could date.

Getting past all the paper and making the kitchen appear as if the gift had thrown up, I paused. Inside was a black bra. I laughed. He bought me a bra?

It was sort of pretty, in a leathery finish, and as I lifted it, I noticed it was slightly heavier than I'd expected.

I turned it around and saw something in the center, the part that would sit against my ribcage. Pulling at the small shiny bit I noticed what it was.

"Well, isn't that clever? A little knife pocket."

Something shifted in the box, and I noticed a card.

It took me a second to wonder why my face was hurting. Realization dawned, I'd never smiled like this before.

I opened the card, and inside was a short message.

Protect what's mine. Parks.

I swallowed. His? Was I? Was he talking about my boobs? I'd taunt him later with that. Maybe. I wasn't sure yet about any of this.

I pulled down the top of the shirt and put the bra on. A perfect fit. Of course it was. He was far too smooth for it not to be. I buttoned the shirt back up. This definitely needed to be tried out.

I still had my boots on. Still had a few knives and now this new accessory. I was going to go out and get a new burner phone and maybe some ice cream. If I had to sit around by myself, I might as well enjoy something. So now, there was the matter of all the cameras.

Walking back into Parks' closet I looked for something I could use. Drawer after drawer, I found lots of wonderful treasures, but none that I needed.

His boxers were all neatly rolled. I snorted. "Control freak." He was far too organized for my tastes, but damn, what he could make me feel.

A few more drawers and I found something of use. Sunglasses. Perfect. Or well, better than nothing.

I got into the elevator and headed downstairs to the lobby. I repeated the same careful walk that it took me to get in here. I remembered that he'd pointed out where each of the cameras were and before I knew it, I was out on the street. Perfect. I looked around and tried to get my bearings.

Directions were not my thing. People? I was great at reading people. Hm. I watched them all walking up and down the street. More men went to my right and more women went to my left. Choices, choices. I watched one man walk. Self-importance dripped from him. I would go his direction. Certainly there was a store somewhere that direction and a bonus if I could meet him. His eyes were hidden behind dark glasses, but I noticed the subtle movement of the whites behind. He'd noticed me and that made my little broken heart beat to a new rhythm. Not the one Parks could inspire, but something alive and real all the same.

Mentally I did a little girl squeal and fell in line.

I walked in and out of people, keeping my distance from him, keeping an eye out for a store as well.

I studied his mannerisms, trying to decide if he was my type or not. It would surprise people if they knew how many skeezy men there were out there. After a few more blocks, I got bored. Something moved out of the corner of my eye, and I decided to follow it down a darker part of the city.

It was still broad daylight, nothing too exciting ever happened in broad daylight. Except maybe my luck was changing.

Someone laughed behind me, and I wasn't surprised. The brick of the alley paired with some stale rotting garbage to set a beautiful scene.

Finally.

Something to do.

"Hey sweetheart, where you going?"

I turned on my toes and faced the talker.

"To the store? You?"

When he smiled, I wrinkled my nose. The guy had a few lines tattooed on his cheek and a few teeth capped or missing.

"I wouldn't smile if I were you. Not until you see a dentist."

His eyes narrowed.

"Shut it bitch. No one asked you."

I heard the steps behind me before I felt the point of something sharp near my kidney.

"Oh good. A friend. Does his smile scare away all the girls too?"

"Bitch he said shut up."

I sighed and waited for one of them to decide what to do.

"Why aren't you screaming?"

I made a little cluck with my tongue before I spoke.

"Why would I do that? No one cares anyway. Haven't you learned people kind of suck?"

They shared a look, or at least I assumed they did. The way he looked over my shoulder told me that he was confused and so was his friend.

"So boys. Are you just protecting this alley or what? I promise I won't be any trouble. Just needing some girl products and stuff. You know."

There was something all villains have in common, most of the time. And I was the worst of the ones in this alley. We weren't predictable.

The cold steel against my side wasn't sure. The hold was weak, and told me he either wasn't into killing me, or this was one of his first times.

"Oh sweetie. You have no idea that your entire day is going to be ruined, do you?"

The guy opened his mouth, and I stopped him.

"It was a rhetorical question, the arrogance on his face told me you had no idea."

My feet moved in compliance of the ape behind me dragging me further into the alley.

"Shut up, bitch."

I sighed. "So this isn't a shortcut then? To the store?"

"Fuck, bitch you talk to damn much."

I had a blade strapped to my forearm, hidden under the cuffed and still too long sleeve of Parks' shirt. It took a shake of my wrist, and both were free. I liked these best.

"I don't like the word bitch, unless we are talking about the mama that raised you."

The guy behind me dropped the knife the second I threw my head back and felt the familiar crunch of a broken nose.

"You didn't fucking do that, bitch."

I turned to see the blood pouring from dude's nose.

"Oh, but I did." I pointed the blade in my hand out and lifted my arm behind me where the guy charging me had no idea. It found soft flesh, but to my dismay, it was his leg. Well, damn it.

"That's it. Fuck you, bitch. Grab her arms," he shouted.

The guy with a broken nose yelled at the guy cursing behind me. He dragged my arms tightly behind my back and it caused a twinge in my shoulder. Not pain though. Never pain.

"I'll show you what we do to bitches."

I gave an obligatory kick or two before the guy behind me yanked my arms and caused me to fall to my knees.

"No. Please. Don't," I said in a flat, emotionless voice. The guy with the broken nose punched me in the temple and I bit my tongue with the impact. It didn't matter. The alley did a quick waver, but it was fine. I was fine. These two were amateurs.

"You won't sound so calm when I'm fucking you, bitch."

I pressed my lips together and let him think he won something.

His nails dragged over my thigh. I sucked in my breath as something else, something cold, pressed between my legs, probably a gun barrel? Hard to say.

"If you don't want to die, you'll stop fighting us."

The guy behind me licked my neck, and I turned so quickly that I caught his lip between my teeth, and I bit down.

Dude in front of me grabbed something, maybe a metal pole? All blunt objects looked the same in shadows. Behind me the guy fell back, and I released his lip. I leaned backwards, away from whatever the other one swung at my head.

He fell off balance and fell into the trash cans.

The guy behind me came and wrapped his hand around my neck and pushed down on my windpipe.

The problem was, he was trying to do something else and wasn't fully committed. Shame. I must have dropped the knives in my hands, but that's okay. I reached for the blade between my breasts, the guy too busy slipping out his dick to think anything else.

Again. Dumb. Parks wasn't dumb. I wondered if I'd met him in an alley, what he could do.

The shift in the air hinted at the dick behind me. I flipped the knife and stabbed at his neck. I got two solid stabs in before he choked and gurgled and fell backwards.

My boot clad foot hit him square in the chest and he stumbled back and down. When I looked back to where the other guy was, or used to be, I shrugged.

He was already running away.

I stood up and blinked.

"Well, now I have a headache. And you ruined my outfit and I'm just pissed off. You won't be needing this anymore."

The guy's hands wrapped around his throat like he could stop the blood from flowing over the hole in his trachea.

His back rested against the brick wall as he slid down. I

reached for his flaccid little dick and sliced it off, tossing it behind me.

"There, a bread crumb for your friend to come find you behind the dumpster. Oh, and because you're a monster. Have you read Frankenstein?"

He couldn't nod or say anything. A bubble of blood kissed his lips as it popped.

"He was soon borne away by the waves and lost in darkness and distance. That's you. Soon you will be lost in the darkness, alone. Carried away by the storm that is me. Okay. Have a great day."

I stood up, and I pressed my hand to my head. Pulling it away, there was blood. Well, damn it. I started to walk, albeit slowly and remembered my sunglasses. I couldn't find them and then I heard a voice.

"Miss? Fuck me. Miss? He's going to kill me. We have to get you back."

THIRTEEN

parks

I WAS GOING to kill someone. I had alerts set for the second that fucking elevator went to my apartment. She shouldn't have been able to fucking get out.

The second I got off the elevator and through the vestibule, my eyes rested on the guard I'd trusted to fucking do as I asked.

"What the fuck was she doing out in the city?"

He tripped over his words, and his face lost all pigment. Good. The fucker would be lucky if I didn't rip his heart out.

"Spit it out, you worthless piece of shit. Where were you while she strolled out the front fucking doors?"

The dude finally found some words.

"I swear I was watching. I had to go to the bathroom though and by that point she'd gotten to the street."

I reached for his throat and squeezed. He knew better than to fight me, and I lost my want to punish him. He was fucking loyal. She was a fucking button pushing, sexy as fuck little minx. It was my own fault for trying to cage her.

"Fuck it. Where is she?"

I dropped him, and he pointed.

The text I'd gotten from this useless sack of shit had sent

tendrils of ice through me. I didn't like the idea that I cared, but from the second I'd seen her I couldn't let her go. I guess it was best to just embrace it.

It would have been so much easier to just kill her and be done. But the one thing in life that was worth living every day for was love, I'd just never understood that until now.

My mother preached that. Hell, the one thing my fucking family believed in was marriage and more family. Power. I protected the family. I was the best at what I did, and I was tied to them by blood. Her? She had spilled that blood.

I should hate her. I shouldn't have had any issues with fucking her and killing her. And yet, I did.

l craved her. I couldn't stop thinking of her. She was a liability. But, being away just made it more clear. Fuck me. She shouldn't have been the one I wanted.

"Halle? Where are you?"

I started towards the bedroom; she could hear me walk in. I was being as subtle as an earthquake.

"You, motherfucker, you are excused," I said over my shoulder.

I didn't even look at him. Just pointed in his direction and didn't give a shit if he crawled or walked to the elevator.

The dark shadow pulling the door open pissed me off even more. Out came Halle, barely fucking dressed.

"What the fuck are you-" I swung around and grabbed the guy that was moving far too slowly. "Get the fuck out, now."

He didn't argue, and I'm sure he was happy to have the help to get out of there and probably relieved I hadn't slit his throat yet.

The second he was out of the apartment I looked back.

"I repeat, what the fuck are you wearing and with another man in this apartment?"

She shrugged, and she didn't bother moving. Just stood there in what? Ah, fuck.

"Is that my gift?"

I flicked on a lamp, keeping the room mostly encapsulated in the dark.

The way her tongue ran over her lip, my cock hardened, and then I ran over the rest of her.

"Where is that bruise from? That asshole didn't hurt you, did he?"

He hadn't said he drug her back here. The text simply said she'd gotten out, and he'd brought her back.

Halle shrugged.

Careful of the angry bruise formed on her arm, I grabbed her waist and walked her backwards, placing her back to the wall and the light where I could see the rest of her body. Her face was so close to mine I could see every single eyelash.

"Where is that bruise from?" I asked again.

This time she rolled her eyes, and I grabbed her chin, forcing her to look up at me.

"Well, I had this great idea to go to the grocery store. Don't worry, I wore sunglasses. Well, for a friendly neighborhood there are a lot of assholes. I mean, sure I shouldn't have cut through the alley. But I did. Anything to stay out of sight like your highness requested."

I liked that she was listening, sort of.

"You just had to call the number and they would bring you food. I don't understand."

She glared at me.

"I am not a kept woman. I need to get out there and do things. Sex is great, but my skin itches with the need to do what I was meant to do."

Fuck. I didn't think about that.

"Okay, we'll circle back. Where is the bruise from?"

She smirked.

"Well, there were two guys in the alley. Whoops. They attacked me."

The entire world disappeared behind red. I closed my eyes to try to control the rage. The wall became my anchor, and I'd be fucking surprised if I didn't dent it.

"They touched what was mine?"

I couldn't see her, but I could feel the way her stomach moved under my hand. I could feel the way she breathed.

"Oh, it's fine. One of them, for sure, isn't ever having kids or raping another girl. Ever. The other? Well, he did get away unfortunately. But I think that will scar him for life."

At this point, there was nothing else that existed besides her and my anger. I was shaking with the need to destroy anything that would touch my woman. My Halle.

Her words filtered in like a God damned brick to the head.

"Wait ever again? Did he fucking rape you?"

She stopped everything and my vision was still clouded in rage, but the feel of her hand on my cheek brought a strange sense of control. A control to hear her.

"Please. Calm down."

I pushed her around the door and into the bedroom. I was gentle enough.

"Lay down on the bed now." My voice was low, and it came out angrier than I'd meant.

When I tried to blink again and clear the anger and rage, what I saw on her face was surprising. There was no fear, just questions.

"Why the bed, oh angry one?"

The hand I had on her waist, I moved and let her go. I shifted my hold from her waist down her hip. There was nothing to stop me. No fabric. No clothing. Just the bra I'd had sent to her. I'd somewhat believed that it was just a kinky bit of lingerie, but truthfully, I hoped that if something or someone ever got to her, she wouldn't be defenseless.

"You said never rape anyone again. Did he touch you? Answer me."

She raised her hand to my chest, and I almost forgot my anger when she smiled. I liked the way she smiled.

"Oh, baby. He tried, he really did, but thanks to your new present I was able to slice his cock off before he could."

My body was still shaking now.

"Get on the bed," I said through clenched teeth.

I dropped my arm from the wall and pushed her toward the bed harder. "Now."

Her eyes sparkled with mischief, that's what I was used to seeing.

I mirrored every step until the back of her legs hit the mattress and she flopped down.

"What is wrong with you? I'm fine, and like I said, he couldn't fuck me if he didn't have a dick. I mean, I left him there to bleed out. I also never got to the grocery store because, well. There was a lot of blood. Who knew-"

I cut her off with a kiss. I wanted to show her I owned her. That every inch of her body was mine and only mine. I crushed my mouth to hers so hard, I would be surprised if I hadn't bruised her.

"No one touches what is mine," I said as I kissed my way down her neck. Her legs spread for me as I slid down onto her.

I pulled the strap of the bra aside looking for more bruises and wasn't disappointed. I snarled as I found each one. I skipped down to between her thighs and paused. I had to force myself to stay here and not go find out who did this. Not yet anyway.

Each bruise and scrape that I saw on her thighs pissed me off, and I kissed each one.

"I will erase this memory. I will fuck you so many times, you won't remember anyone's hands on you ever. Except for mine."

I kissed my way over her soft skin, my fingers playing over her soft pussy, sliding down the slit. I wanted to taste her. Taste every sweet drop of her orgasm as she came for me and only me.

"I will make you scream my name until you forget that there is anyone else in this world," I growled out as my tongue darted between the lips of her sweet, slick pussy. I licked up her slit and stopped at the little nub. I flicked it and circled it just the way I knew she liked. I parted her wider with my thumbs so I could lick her, all of her.

Within moments I could hear her breathing grow more rapid and her muscles in her thighs tighten. I teased her more and when her fingers tangled in my hair, I brought two fingers to her entrance, running them just around the edges. Wetting them from her arousal. I thrust my fingers inside her as a moan escaped her beautiful mouth.

My fingers inside her and my mouth on her clit, I stroked her and worked her and pushed her until she cried out.

"Parks, yes. Don't. Stop."

Her words were choppy, and I knew she was close. I added a third finger into her tightness.

"God, you taste so good," I said between lapping at her core and licking her clit.

I crooked my fingers inside her and stroked her, stroked the even more sensitive spot inside her, and at the same time I pressed my thumb to her clit adding pressure as I worked her.

Within seconds her body trembled, and her core pulsed around my fingers, and I could feel her coming. Could feel the wetness spilling around my hand.

I let her come down from it, and then pulled my fingers out and moved to her mouth.

"Think of this while I go do something quickly. I will be back."

Her eyes flew open.

"What? No, you fucking don't."

I narrowed my gaze.

"I need to go take care of this first."

She snarled at me and then without warning, she locked her leg around me and pushed me over with her entire body, landing with her on top.

She looked down on me and fuck me if the crazy in those gorgeous baby blues wasn't enough to make me hard.

"You take care of me first," she said. She gyrated her hips over my pants.

"No, I will go hunt down the assholes who touched what is mine."

She rolled her eyes at me, and I couldn't wait for the sass.

"Fuck you. I am not yours. And two, you don't play with my pussy and then walk away without giving me your dick. I want to be filled and fucked until I can't walk. Then, I can dream of you torturing those assholes and imagine what you will look like splattered in their blood. But now? Make me forget they exist."

halle

WHY WAS I just sitting here on his couch flipping through every streaming service that I didn't even know existed? Richard sat on my shoulder eating a pepper slice I held for him while I flipped through more channels. I didn't even own a TV, but here I had nothing to do.

It had been an entire two days since I'd tried to get out and get a job. Well, a phone to get a job. I was getting restless, and he knew that. Parks knew it, but it didn't stop the fact I had a furious and grumpy looking guard watching the elevator.

No one knew my name it appeared. I was just his kept woman. He got me another phone, a real one. One I couldn't use for work because it would lead back to me. Annoying. I sent a text.

I need to get out and check out a book.

I watched waiting for a response, nothing. I flopped over, careful of Richard. I should just make a run for it. What would he do? I sighed and handed Richard a bit of melon. He'd hunt me down again.

This sucked. Well not totally sucked, but a lot sucked.

It sucked to be wanted.

There were expectations. One? That you would actually come back to them. I think maybe that was fair. I could get used to this. Go out kill someone and then come back to sex.

My body seemed to like this idea as the heat pooled between my legs.

I wore a simple little dress that had pockets. Parks had sent some things for me. Or rather, boxes and boxes of things. What kind of fucking world did I walk into?

I checked my phone again. Nothing.

I flipped off the TV and grabbed Richard and a couple more snacks that we'd been sharing before putting him back into his cage.

From there I paced. I couldn't do this. I texted him again.

If you don't take me out soon, I'm leaving.

Would I leave? Sure. I would go back to old me. Flip my switch and forget him. Feeling a whole lot of nothing was easy. So easy. Did I care if he would miss me? I paced some more. Would I? Wait, would I miss him?

It had been a mistake to come here in the first place. I'd let myself get caught, and this guy? So much more dangerous than the cops.

But really? Why had I? The guy gave me a fun gift and I was his? That wasn't normal. Was it? And then I just laughed like a crazy person. Or, well, the crazy person I once shared a room with. Maybe I understood her now.

What the ever-loving hell was normal?

A few minutes later, I stopped pacing and flopped on the bed this time. I would leave. It was fine. He would be fine. We'd been fine. I would be fine. I just needed my work. The adrenaline of finding a new target excited me, and instead of staying focused on the body I dreamed of, the one I didn't have a face for yet, Parks invaded my fantasy.

God. No. Why couldn't I forget him? Just to know that night, the one where he took me on a date, that he was with me? It had felt amazing. It was so hot to know he was in the same apartment as me doing God knew what to that woman. Fuck. We had been there together. And those two, a match made in hell, got to die together. It was so romantic.

My hands slid between my legs remembering how Parks had touched me afterwards. I needed to take the edge off of my crazy. God, it was too damn much. His big powerful hands knew how to bring pleasure and pain and I wanted to walk that line with him.

My body was so hot, and my pussy ached to be touched.

I pulled the skirt of my dress up. The fabric waking nerves that only Parks could truly bring alive. Nothing was as good as his touch, but I ran my fingers over the same trail that he would have kissed and caressed. I played at my folds, pretending it was him spreading me, heading straight for my clit.

I stroked myself, slowly at first, until the heat inside me grew and an electric flutter vibrated through me as I tried to get myself closer and closer.

God, Parks covered in blood was fucking hot. One less fucking assshole in the world trying to hurt someone?

"Oh, God," I said on a breath.

Someone cleared their throat, and I paused. Oh, I'd forgotten there was a guard down a small hall. Perhaps he— I paused and smirked as I looked into familiar eyes.

"I thought you were threatening to leave? This? This would have gotten me home so much faster."

The look on his face as he took me in.

"How was your day?" I asked.

He growled.

"Better now. Spread your legs for me," he commanded. He moved like a panther and was on the bed spreading me before I could breathe in.

I sucked in a breath as his tongue licked up my slit, doing everything in one delicious motion that I had been trying to do all by myself.

Something I never thought I would feel, let alone crave, was the way the warmth of tingling nerves covered your entire body. He kissed up and down my body, pushing the dress higher and higher.

The dress caught just under my nose, and I was blinded to him as he claimed my mouth while he held my arms above my head.

"You do not bait me, princess. What happened to you being a good little girl? Haven't I fucked you good? I promise, I will take you out soon."

His hand slid over my braless breasts. I had put little effort into what I wore, except for the dress to make sure I never got in trouble for being naked at least. But this?

"I need out now," I said between each breath that caught in my lungs at each of his surprising touches.

"Now, now, Rainbow. It takes time. I need this next one to be perfect."

I arched my back into him as his mouth closed on my nipple. His teeth dragged against the sensitive nub, and I wanted more. I wanted all of him.

"If you won't take me out, then make me forget, asshole. Make me forget what a complete fucking control freak you are."

My entire body was vibrating with the unmet need. He'd walked in and denied me an orgasm and now I needed him to shut the hell up and I got my request, but with a price.

I didn't know what was coming. His tongue licked a path. His lips left me hungry for his touch. Something wrapped around my wrists, I wasn't getting this dress off. His weight shifted and his hand cupped my heat. His fingers played with my entrance and yet I was robbed of the release again.

"Fuck me," I begged. I pushed against his hand and yet, nothing.

"You threaten to leave me, and I come home to you without any panties. No bra. And my guard just outside the main living space. What should I do with you?"

The backs of his fingers trailed over my thighs and kept missing my pussy. I moaned, wanting him to touch me more.

Anything. My breasts ached. How did he do this?

For someone that thought she was fucking broken and numb, he was finding new ways to wake up parts of me I didn't know could be.

"I'm bored. What do you want me to do all day?" I hated the way my voice sounded. But I couldn't see him. I couldn't do anything but feel.

"Do all day? Wait for me." He licked me. "Trust me." He kissed up my stomach.

"Trust you?"

He paused the kissing and the licking.

"Have I broken your trust yet?"

I thought about it.

"I mean, stalking isn't exactly a trustworthy trait, is it?"

I felt his chest vibrate against me. He was laughing.

"No, I suppose it isn't. Well, then perhaps we start from after the stalking."

His hands glided up my sides, sending chills over me.

"Did I not save you from getting caught?" More kisses, and he was so close to my breasts, I wiggled trying to get him to move the dress. I want to feel his mouth against my nipples, feel the bite of his teeth.

"Did I not find you someone fun and interesting to take you on a date with?"

I groaned at the feel of the graze of his teeth, teasing me.

"Did I not give you gifts that you desired?"

Gifts. Oh yes, the gifts. The syringe and the bra.

"Did I not go get you dick?"

I giggled at that. The giggle turned into whimpers.

I could feel the crown of his big, beautiful cock against my slit. Every little twitch. Every breath I took seemed to flex my muscles and rub against him.

"Have I not given you many, many orgasms? Always making sure you get yours?"

I pressed my head against the bed, still unable to see, still unable to kiss him at my own will.

"Yes, always."

I almost begged for him to take me, but before I could find the first syllable, he thrust into me on one long hard movement and all I could think of was how fucking good he felt inside me.

I'd be mad later.

parks

HALLE WAS GOING STIR CRAZY, I knew it, but I had to work. It twisted me inside out to think of keeping her from what she needed. I realized it was her therapy.

It twisted me more to think of letting her go. I didn't know what to do about my family as of yet, but I needed her to be happy first.

The wild in her eyes was tamed after one or two or five orgasms. But it wouldn't be enough, it wasn't enough. I wasn't enough alone. She was lucky I'd share her with the same passion I had.

So, that left me with only one option, and letting her out made things messy.

My uncle had been ranting for days. I already knew what all the meetings were about. He was worried about the family, more threats. More players in other cities. I just needed to do the dirty work when negotiations failed. Which might work out for my next plan.

I was back to thinking of the woman in my bed. On one hand, I think she would come home to me because I was fairly certain she'd become just as addicted to me as I was to her. On the other hand, I risked not only her life, but possibly mine as well if somehow things got out.

I should have just killed her instead of watching her. It had just taken so fucking long to find her, that the idea of having to kill her once I saw her work, well. It seemed slightly anticlimactic. Like I needed some kind of fanfare for killing her. She deserved a fucking parade for being so fucking sexy and so incredibly fucked up.

I kissed her temple as she lay in my arms. I was new to having a woman in my bed. I would never tell her that I wasn't new to women, but having them in my space? That was new. If you kept a woman around to long, they got clingy. If they got clingy, the rich ones got daddy to start marriage arrangements. The poor ones started to think that I was a god to be worshiped. I was no hero, not of their stories anyway.

To my Halle? I'd try anyway. Funny thing heroes. Sometimes the villain was the hero. It just depended on who was telling the story I supposed.

She made a little whimper in her sleep. It wasn't the first time. With it came a tossing and turning and a spiked heartbeat. It wasn't me in there, that was for sure.

I reached over and pulled her in against my chest. This seemed to help. Not in a million years had I ever given two shits what fucking helped anyone. Caring was baggage, and my family gave me enough to last a lifetime of therapy sessions, although I had no intention of ever going to get myself fixed.

I knew my issues. I killed people. That in itself was probably an issue. But Halle? Her moral code was fantastic and confusing. Killing my cousin instead of the mark he hired her for? Not an awful choice. But how did she decide who was the more rotten of the two?

He'd been an idiot hiring outside the family. You think he would have known better. I didn't know that I cared how his death happened even when we got the news, or I should say when my uncle got the parts of him.

A few more minutes of holding her. That's all I needed. This was breaking from my normal and I think I liked it. Instead of heading to go work out, which is what I did when sleep seemed impossible, I was choosing to lay here with her. This seemed better. Calmer. I could work out another time. Halle stirred, and I looked down meeting her gorgeous green eyes.

"Awake then?"

She shifted, and I wasn't loosening my grip.

"I am, and I need to go to the bathroom."

She wiggled out. It felt strongly empty without her.

"I enjoy watching you walk around naked, perhaps that should be the new rule. No clothes when I'm home."

She smiled at me, and the sway of her hips seemed to be exaggerated, making my cock stand erect. Fuck. She had no idea what she did to me.

I had no idea what she was doing to me. I wanted to get my hands on her. Right now.

It was early, which meant we had some time. We still had a couple of hours before the plane was scheduled to take off, and I hadn't told her yet. It was a surprise, and I hoped she liked it.

Now, for my morning wake up routine. Tossing the blankets aside, I headed for the bathroom and stood in the doorway just watching her. She noticed and tried to throw whatever she could grab at me.

"What did that towel ever do to you?"

She growled at me.

"Get out."

I shrugged and stood there in all my glory.

"Nope. Time for a shower."

I walked around her and started the shower. I had several rainfall heads, a bench for the sauna option, and several other options I'd never actually bothered using. I'd never given two shits about the fancy shower, to be fair. But put her in there and it was my favorite spot. Everywhere she was became my favorite spot, which is what led me to today's adventures.

"I'm waiting," I said, running my hands through my hair letting the water run down my body.

Small, cold hands gripped my ass, and I smiled.

"Took you long enough."

I reached behind me and pulled her around, planting a kiss on her. My cock throbbed already. Fuck I was like a teenager, hungry for sex any way I could get it.

"It's about time you got in here," I said, and bent down to her mouth.

She was so much shorter than me like this, and it didn't matter as I grabbed her ass and lifted her.

"Wrap your legs around me and hold on," I said against her ear.

Her breathing grew more rapid, and her breasts rose and fell, my mouth descending on a taut nipple. She was just as hungry as I was.

I pressed her back against the wall, loving every taste of her as I licked at her skin.

"Fuck me, Parks. Make me feel alive."

The warmth of her pussy against the head of my shaft fueled my own fire. My hands dug into her soft skin, and I rubbed her body against mine, feeling the give of her core as I stretched her over my thickness took me to a whole new level of pleasure.

I waited for her to react each time I thrust deep inside her. I pressed into her, holding her to me, letting her feel every inch of my body in hers, teasing her. Her breath caught several times as I shifted, and I loved the sound. I loved the feel of her nails biting into my shoulders as she tensed, ready for me to retreat and slam back into her. But instead I kissed her, waiting for her to relax, and then I would take her again and again.

I pulled out again and teased her entrance, letting my head slick against her, letting her need coat me, letting myself slide through her folds, hitting her clit and making her release some of the sweetest little sounds.

I was getting close to breaking though. I didn't want to wait, and I didn't need to.

With a swift, quick motion I slammed into her, and she gasped and then moaned.

I nearly came at the sweet tightness of her core as I stretched her wide with every thrust.

"Fuck. I can't get enough of your tight little cunt," I ground out as I lifted her again and let her slam back down onto my rock-solid cock.

Over and over I let gravity do the work, and then it was my turn. I wanted control and I took it. I gripped her hard and pinned her between me and the wall, and I pushed into her harder and faster making her come for me.

She would come for me. I wouldn't allow her not to. And I didn't.

"Oh, God. Parks."

Her words, breathless and needy and everything my fucking cock wanted to hear because, as she was still pulsing around me, swallowing me and taking from me, I slammed in one more time and came.

We stood there together, catching our breath and feeling our bodies pressed hot together.

"Alright, princess. Get dressed in something nice. I have a surprise for you."

SIXTEEN

"YOU HAVE a big screen TV on a plane? And a bar? And a couch?"

I waved my champagne around, trying to take it all in. "I am definitely upping my fees."

Parks didn't talk, the way he peered over his phone told me he thought this was entertaining. I shifted in my seat to look outside at all the water. My clients weren't international, but damn. They should be.

"Maybe I should be charging you?" I said, more to myself than to him.

He rolled his eyes. "Aright, Halle. What services do you want to charge me for?"

I took a sip and thought about it. Perhaps I should just make him help me set up a better business model. Nah. This was way more fun.

"Where should I start? Loss of business? Oh, use of my girly parts seems a little unfair since you really seem to need the sex to be a decent person. But, then again, that's like therapy or something. I'll google therapy rates later."

Nothing about him said what he was thinking. But the tap,

tap, tap of his finger on the chair told me he was thinking at least.

"You want me to pay you for sex? Is it not enough that I am taking you on a business trip?"

I pressed my lips. "Well, it depends. What is the business we're tripping to?"

He handed me an iPad with a news article and a photo. I shrugged.

"Corporate greed?"

He took it away and tapped something else.

"That is the part that concerns my family. The part that you will enjoy is his background and where he got his money."

I took one last sip of the bubbly liquid and put the glass down.

"So, is it the pot calling the kettle black then? I don't think your family is exactly on the moral highroad. Don't get me wrong, for the most part I don't care. Except your cousin. I cared about him. You don't hire a girl and then send her dick pics."

His brow rose. "How in the hell did you meet my cousin that he was able to send dick pics?"

I smiled.

"I mean, I have my ways. One is dressing up all slutty like and cruising bars. Men talk when they are drunk. Not all my work is from the library. That's just the up and up stuff."

Parks didn't say anything for a few seconds.

"Okay. Well, this gentleman has recently caused my family some public issues. In the past six months, properties that he's rented from us have become speculation for sex trafficking.

Parks sent back the iPad and this time there were images that were not news articles.

"That girl? She's—"

I cut him off.

"Say no more. So we get to play with him?"

He nodded.

"I know it's hard for you not to be free. You talk a bit in your sleep."

I threw a decorative pillow at him.

"I do not."

He stood from his seat and leaned over mine.

"How would you know?" And kissed me. "Now, I am going to go speak with the pilot. Food will be delivered shortly."

And he walked away. From my position I was able to watch him walk away. My heart skipped in excitement and even contentment.

I needed this. I needed to let my demons out before they could consume me, his ass wasn't hurting though. The sex helped. Perhaps in another life, I'd have made a different career choice. When I laughed at the idea and how Parks would react if I suggested selling myself, well my drink was up my nose.

I paused and watched him talk to the female flight attendant. No. I would never have chosen another profession.

I imagined cutting her up into tiny little pieces and dropping them out of the plane just for the way she looked at my Parks. I narrowed my gaze. Yes, cutting her up would serve me well and she'd still get to see the world, now, wouldn't she?

I cleared my throat. "Hey, waitress?"

She startled and turned my way. I don't think she was dumb enough to show anyone disrespect on this plane, but it wasn't like she knew me.

"Yes, miss?"

I nodded my head and pointed after Parks. "That man?"

She nodded. "Mr. Rossi?"

I huffed. "Yes. Mr. Rossi. He has a great ass, doesn't he?"

She giggled. "Oh my god. The best."

I grabbed the lapel of the white button-down shirt she was wearing.

"Great. Look at it again and I will make sure that it will be the last thing you see as you free fall a few thousand feet to—" I paused and looked out the window.

"Hmm, looks like an ocean. Did you know that when you hit water at high speeds it feels just like concrete? You'd be amazed what a body looks like when it hits concrete."

I could hear her swallow and then heard the cockpit door open. I let her go.

"So, what do you say? Are we besties now?"

Her eyes were like saucers. I assume that was a no, but I think I got my point across.

"What are you two up to? Is the food ready?"

I appreciated the look she gave me before turning to go back to the front of the plane.

"What did you do?" he asked.

I shrugged.

"I don't like her."

I could hear the breath he took.

"I'm pretty sure we can fill an entire cemetery with the bodies of everyone you don't like. What did you do to my help?"

I crossed my arms, making my breasts rise to the occasion. Perhaps I could use this to my advantage. The lower cut of the dress's neckline has seemed useless until now.

"Well, she looked at you wrong." I tried to get the girly whine just right.

It wasn't working. I don't think he was going to laugh, but the corner of his mouth twitched.

"Halle, drop the act. Are you jealous? Why do you think I've fucked someone who works for my family?"

Well, now I just felt challenged, and I didn't like that anymore than whatever was happening. Jealousy? I didn't feel jealous, except...

"Parks, it's been too long since I was able to let my demons out. This isn't my fault."

I could feel the world getting a little smaller and the air growing a bit thicker.

"Calm down, princess. It's okay."

It wasn't okay, though. I needed to let it all out, or I was going to lose control of what kept me normal. Or, well, whatever my normal was.

"I promise you, this will all be worth it. Now just breathe for me."

I didn't want to, though. I didn't really truly know how to. Not without my work to ground me.

Parks picked me up and moved us to the back of the plane, not that it was leaps and bounds far away, but it did seem to have a little more privacy.

"Hold the food until the curtains open," Parks said, and unfastened the curtain behind us. It created something close to a door.

"Come here."

He kissed me, slowly at first, letting me decide what I wanted. Was this going to be enough? Kissing? Never. Him?

I pushed my hips against him because I needed more.

SEVENTEEN

parks

SHE WENT from kissing me to me restraining her hands before she punched me again.

"Calm down," she repeated.

I'd given her a lot of rules lately and I could see it was cracking away at her self-control. A control she'd been barely hanging onto for a lifetime.

Fuck me. What the hell was I doing? I should have just finished the job. Taken her out at that shithead's house. The clean-up crew had been told two bodies and yet, there had been one. I'd spent a brutally annoying afternoon having to explain why my uncle was told there was only one body, and it wasn't female.

But then, holding her in my arms. I didn't want easy. I wanted Halle.

The way Halle looked up at me right now, showing me the only clue to who else was in there other than the crazy dark-side I'd fallen for first, this was why I'd allowed my uncle to question my integrity.

My uncle was a sick fuck, and I suppose you had to be to run the biggest mob on this coast. Still, convincing him to let me

106

play with her more wasn't easy, until I'd gotten the best distraction yet. The one that I was taking her to now. I'd tracked down my uncle's ex-best friend. This would distract him for quite some time.

"What are you thinking, Halle?"

I knew what she was thinking. My cock grew hard just at the way she looked at me. My family had stories about marrying for power instead of love. That the wrong women could be the end of the Rossi family. But Halle? My twisted rainbow?

She fucked with her eyes just as good as she did with her pussy.

"Princess, don't threaten my staff anymore. My cock doesn't care for any of them, regardless of any history. I only want you."

I couldn't listen to anymore of her crazy, not today. I kissed her lips to shut her up. I was in denial that it was to quench my own craving for her.

Her hands were calm and quick, and one was down my pants. Her soft, delicate fingers clasped over my cock. Fuck me, it felt amazing. Who was owning who?

I grabbed her up, turning us and sitting down on the couch with her astride me.

"Rainbow, you do that any longer and I'm going to lose my patience. There won't be any licking your cunt until you're begging for me to come inside you."

I wasn't winning this one.

"You can do that later. Right now? I want to make sure that I've fucked you so good, that that bitch could strip naked in front of you, and you wouldn't be able to get it up."

She kissed my neck and unzipped my pants.

"Fuck, you're crazy, princess."

My hands wrapped in the dress she was wearing.

Between every kiss she gave me more of her little twisted

plan that didn't really seem necessary. But, then again, I sure as shit wasn't saying no to her. Ever.

"I want to fuck you so good that my thighs glisten with your release and you can't not see it every time I uncross my legs."

I grew harder with every word she spoke.

"I want to fuck you so hard that every cry from my lips is louder than the engines of this plane, and it makes her so fucking horny that she has to take care of herself listening to every moan escaping your lips as you bury yourself deep inside me."

The further I got under her skirt, the less there was any reason to deny what she was demanding.

"Fuck, Rainbow. No panties?"

She smirked. "It would have been so much harder to do this had I worn them, don't you agree?"

I licked my lips and swallowed.

She leaned forward, her breasts peeking over the neckline of the soft clingy fabric I'd asked her to wear.

"Now, Parks. Fuck me and tell her exactly who you belong to."

She pushed my pants further down and I shifted, allowing them down my thighs. I slid my hand down her inner thigh, and fucking loved the feel of her already slick folds as I slid down her pussy.

"Halle, I think you're mistaken as to who belongs to who."

I pressed my thumb over her clit, and her entire body seemed to shiver.

"Now, shut up and fuck me," I said.

She rose over me, and I guided my thick shaft until I felt the heat of her entrance over the head of my cock.

I grabbed her lower back with one arm and her hip with my now free hand.

"Show me, princess. How much do you want to make her jealous?"

I had to keep myself controlled as her beautiful pussy stretched around my rock-solid hard-on.

I held her there before I could sink in deeper, before she could push me deeper.

"Tell me, Halle. Who belongs to who?"

She wiggled in my grip.

"You belong to me, Parks. Now fuck me."

My grip tightened, and I watched the pupils of her eyes dilate.

"Now, now. You know that's the wrong answer. You want my cock to make you scream? You want her to hear you scream as you come for me? As you pulse around me? Be a good girl."

I let her sink a little further down and I swear my own pulse tripled.

"You want more?"

Her teeth bit into her bottom lip. As she released it, I could see every little divot that her teeth left.

"Fine. I'm yours. But you're mine too. And if you don't fuck me soon, I'm going to go on a killing spree and it's going to start with cutting off every fucking finger of those perfectly mani-cured hands so she can never touch you."

I pulled her down and she let out the loudest groan; there was no doubt the entire plane could hear what we were doing.

She lifted herself, and I let her. I let her set the rhythm as she took control and fucked me the way she wanted. Until I could hear her heart thundering and see her eyes glaze over the closer she neared to her release. I wouldn't let her come, not unless it was from me.

I grabbed her, my dick still buried inside, and dropped her to the couch. In one seamless motion, I was thrusting into her again and again, and in seconds, the walls of her pussy were pulsing around my cock. Now it was my turn.

I thrust inside her so hard and so fast, driven by the frantic rhythm of breathless and intelligible sounds coming from her mouth.

The way she screamed again I knew she was coming all over again, and I loved the slick pool of her release around me and the quiver of her entire body. I slammed into her one more time and this time I let myself come.

She would have my come down her legs, but the other side of it would be that she would be marked by me even as we got to the party tonight.

EIGHTEEN

"BYE, babe. So great to have you serve us."

I gave that bitch a finger wave as Parks practically dragged me down the stairs onto the tarmac.

"What?" I whined.

He pulled me closer, wrapping my waist with his arm.

"Do not play with her. She has had enough of a show from you."

I giggled and tried to break away from him, to give myself space, but he pulled me against him harder.

"Do not stray far princess. This is no longer my territory, and these men do not play nice."

I pulled in the scent of wherever we were.

"It sort of smells like the ocean. Where are we?" I enjoyed the heat over my body. This was somewhere tropical.

"Is this an island?"

A car was waiting for us, and as we got close, the driver stepped out.

"Wow. Do you get this kind of service everywhere you go? I'm definitely charging more."

He didn't react, not even a little. He had a hard set to his face, here he seemed to be stony and cold. This must be his business face.

Here he seemed different. The way his hand slid down the low, open back of the dress I changed into on the plane though? It was just as hot and possessive.

"Sir. Miss."

I didn't say anything, mostly because he was manhandling me inside the car. Once the door closed, he grabbed me and pulled me onto his lap.

"Alright, Rainbow. I am working, as are you. Know that my enemies are vast, and whereas you are invisible to most of yours, mine know me."

I ran a finger over his chin.

"Well, that's because I kill all of mine," I said.

This time, I know he chuckled.

"Yes. That would be ideal, but in this line of work, enemies and allies can sometimes be one in the same, and sometimes that means leaving certain players alive."

I pursed my lips.

"Not today though, right?"

He pulled me closer as the car took off.

"Not today. And that's where you come in. This guy, he knows he's in deep shit. No one knows who you are. We're heading to a party at his mansion. He will be intrigued by you because everything we have, he wants."

I put a finger over his lips.

"Wait. Wait. Wait. He knows he's in deep shit and he's having a party?"

His massive hand wrapped around my wrist and pulled my finger away but not before sucking on it.

"Yes, princess. Sometimes, people in power tend to think they are untouchable. He is expecting me, and me, he can watch, so that is where you come in."

I sucked in the air as his hand slid up the slit in the dress I wore.

It went higher and higher and fuck me. Sex was almost enough to keep my demons at bay, or at least keep me tired enough to not be needy.

"Good. You put on the panties."

I glared as he pulled his hand down.

"You told me it was a matter of my life or his. I really want to kill him, so I did what you asked."

Not that the panties were much more than a g-string. But whatever, if it made him happy.

I closed my eyes and let him finish his inspection. The dress was tight, like nothing I would normally have worn. Black tie appropriate. But for him and his enemies? I'd try it all out. What that meant in addition to this dress? He had a custom corset made for me and his hands slid over it. I shivered and wished for an encore of the show on the plane.

"All three knives are in place it appears."

I opened my eyes.

"Can I inspect you now?"

I turned around and straddled him.

"I'm going to start with here," and I ran my hands over his chest, down his pecs, to his sides just below the armpit. One single, slight bulge met my fingers. I kept going, and this time he closed his eyes. I got lower and lower, and enjoyed the way his muscles tensed under my touch as I checked every inch of his junk and his thighs. Lower and lower.

"Hmm. Okay. I guess you have knives in all the normal places. This though," and I grabbed his cock again. "This is my favorite weapon. It somehow gets me to do anything you ask."

He cocked a brow.

"Anything? Then why don't you ever seem to behave?"

I shrugged. "Oh, that's never going to happen. So now,

where do I fit in this plan?" I shifted over to the seat next to him and looked outside. Indeed, water. An island, maybe? It was hard to tell. Maybe whenever we left, I'd actually look out the window of the plane this time. Maybe. Doubtful.

"The plan, princess. You get in, find him, and seduce him away from the crowd."

That got my attention.

"Seduce him, huh? You don't mind another man touching me?"

He shifted.

"Princess, seduce him to get him alone. Do not touch him."

I looked back out the window and noticed the sun setting. Wherever we were, it was getting late.

"Fine. Whatever you need babe."

I flexed my hands over and over without realizing it until the warmth of his hands slid into mine.

"Are you nervous?"

He kissed my knuckles.

"What? No. I just need to take the edge off. It's been too long, and I really am about to lose it. That or you can fuck me again, but I need this."

He didn't say anything for a while. But as we wound a mountainous road, his fingers brushed my cheek.

"I don't know who hurt you princess. But someday they will pay. For now? Let's go do as you said. Take the edge off. Be careful."

The car climbed a hill, and by now the darkness was finding home among the mountains, or maybe it was the shadows. Either way, the house at the top of the hill was anything but discreet. Lights on in every window.

"How big of a party is this?"

Out the window, I could make out the silhouette of parked cars.

"He's an idiot," was all Parks said.

I couldn't agree more.

As the car pulled up to the door of the ostentatious mansion, I took a glance back at Parks as the driver opened my door. He nodded, and I slid out. The dress blew in a silky drape around my legs as the sea breeze greeted us.

I took a step forward, taking in the place. Most people were inside, with a few that appeared on a balcony that I suspected looked out to the ocean, but from the driveway the view was obstructed.

Parks' hand slid over my lower back.

We walked in together, but I looked around for any exits.

"Princess?"

I turned my face up, and he pulled me in close to hear him whisper.

"Yes?"

He nodded at my chest. "That necklace, there's a gift inside. And just remember. Seduce him, but you belong to me."

All I could offer was a little smirk. I did what I wanted, and he knew that, and I would do whatever it took to get what I needed. Another asshole dead. Even if it wasn't someone I wanted dead, I would play this game. A bad guy was a bad guy. Right now? I looked like some rich bitch, and it was always fun to be someone else. Maybe this was how one got higher class clients.

I walked away from Parks and grabbed a glass of champagne, downing it in one quick gulp while I scanned the room. *Oh where, oh where is my little mouse?*

The room was beautiful, over the top, and screamed sociopath. I would know. I glanced behind me, but I didn't need to. Park's eyes burned a hole through me. Through this dress. This was good though. Here the guy couldn't let his freak flag fly. No little girls in sight.

Just a woman, wanted by his rival. This should be easy.

I watched eyes in the room. Watched for the guy who looked like the images Parks showed me. One face at a time. The good news was, I was pretty sure that several of the men and women here would make a great alternative if I couldn't find this guy.

I sighed and grabbed another glass, as yet another server passed in front of me. I could still feel Park's gaze on me as I stayed in the strange area that was raised before two steps led down into what was apparently the ballroom. I could blend in with the rich, it didn't mean I needed to understand them.

"Ciao principessa," said an unfamiliar voice.

I crossed my arms over my chest and slowly turned to him.

"I'm sorry. I don't speak Italian."

The good news: I could cross Italy off my bucket list. The bad news: this wasn't the guy.

"I'm looking for someone."

I worked to make sure my resting bitch face couldn't be misconstrued.

"Ah, an American," said another voice, and this time something in my gut told me he was the right one.

The guy in front of me seemed to be retreating far too fast for the man behind me not to be important and somewhat intimidating.

"Yes, and by the little accent you are not," I said as I finally faced him.

He was older, silver hair and laugh lines. But mostly, he was very good looking if you were into sugar daddies. That was useless for him tonight. And it had been a curse for so many girls, I was certain of that.

"I am both a citizen in the US and here."

I didn't bother asking where here was. He continued to talk and bore me, but I had a part to play.

"Oh, that's so exotic," I crooned.

He glared over my shoulder towards where I'd left Parks.

"Shall we get to know each other out of the line of prying eyes?"

I batted my eyes and giggled or some such shit. It was all too easy to manipulate him.

"Sure. Is there somewhere more quiet? There're so many people here."

I giggled and did a little trip. "Whoopsie. Looks like I've had too much wine already."

He shrugged. "Don't worry. I'll make sure to help you. But perhaps, well, will your company miss you?" he asked looking around.

I took another sip of the champagne.

"Oh, no. My aunt and uncle don't even seem to remember they brought me."

He nodded.

"Ah. Aunt and Uncle."

He would continue to fish for information, they always did. I would continue to be coy and mysterious.

"That quiet place? My head is just spinning."

A strange twinkle in his eyes lit up his face, and I was certain I'd said exactly the right thing to make his party just that much better.

parks

HE WAS A PREDICTABLE ASSHOLE. I watched Halle out of the corner of my eye, and he noticed. Of course he did. He always wanted what my family had. Or what my family wanted. He knew me, and I'm sure he was curious as to why I had made him aware of my visit.

False sense of security. Just like the girl that he was snaking his arm around.

My nails bit into the palm of my hand. I needed to remain calm. It was okay. This was the plan. But fuck, what a fucking stupid plan. Take her on a job. I had thought it would fix two problems. Her cabin-fever that was growing more and more apparent, as well as an easy way to separate him from the herd.

Make it seem like I didn't know her but show interest. That was the easiest way. But seeing him touching her?

Fuck me. I quickly pushed through the crowd, avoiding attention where I could. I needed to keep her in my sight.

They were getting further and further down a hall that led to his private quarters, away from the prying eyes.

Fuck. I hung back until they turned a corner far ahead of

where I was and no longer where I could even attempt to hear them.

I quickly followed and hung back at the junction. The little sound of her laughing echoed and set my heart on fire. She was laughing at something he said, but it wasn't real. I knew it wasn't real, but fuck, it almost sounded real. I knew her laugh though and this one? It was dripping in anger.

The sound of her heels against the tile grew further away, and I peeked around the corner. Fuck they'd turned again.

I raced to catch up, trying to keep her where I could see her. I told myself it was safety. And it was. But I knew she could handle herself. It was more because I wanted to watch her. Maybe help her.

I was in so much trouble.

Fuck.

I wasn't going to admit it.

I slowed down, and realized the lack of security. He was in financial ruin, but the lack of security surprised me. Big lavish party and yet he wasn't taking care of himself?

I followed along until I heard the click of a door close. Fuck. Where were they? There were several options, and I listened at each door. I found it strange that not a single person guarded his halls still. He was pompous and arrogant. They were all at the front door or around the party. There was a show of his power there and it was small and unimposing.

He would regret his choices.

I walked around and listened. She would be talking, it would be obvious where they were.

Finally, behind door number three I heard something. A whimper? Fuck, I couldn't be sure. It had only been a few seconds. A minute tops.

The metal of the doorknob was cold in my hand. I wanted to

avoid any notice and slowly turned it. The door opened a crack in my hand.

The crack was all I needed to set my demons free. My face burned as I saw what the noise was. He had his hands on her ass as he kissed her. He was moaning as she allowed him to touch her.

Fuck this.

I threw the door open and walked towards him, grabbing him by the neck.

"What the fuck?" I screamed at her and then him.

He glared.

"She came with me willingly, Rossi. Leave us be. Don't make me call my guards."

This time it was my turn to laugh.

Call his guards.

"I wouldn't call anyone if I were you," and I stabbed him in the neck, but careful to keep the main arteries intact.

An angry punch landed against my arm, and I looked down as I dropped him to his knees. Fuck me. I'd promised her that she could kill him.

"Look, I'm sorry. He touched you. He won't die though, not yet. You can still play. Make him pay. Here."

I pulled out a skein of rope from the lined pocket of my jacket.

"What? Pink rope and I'm supposed to be all happy again? I didn't even get to make him scream. You took that away from me."

I shifted towards him; the blood starting to slow a bit. He was in pain, but he would live, until she got to him.

"He won't be screaming loudly, Princess. But since you failed to use my little gift, I had to do something."

She stomped her foot. "No you didn't. I hadn't gotten there yet. I had the move all planned. Drop the necklace into his glass slightly cracked to let the powder mix. But instead—"

I couldn't take it anymore. Every single word she said was muted by the anger of seeing his lips on hers. I grabbed her chin and pulled her lips to mine.

She was the one to pull away, and it pissed me off. Was he a better kisser?

Halle glared at me and then turned to him.

"Oh dear. It looks like I have to cut our playtime short. So, tell you what. Let's play a game. If you can tell me which book this quote is from, you get to die quickly, and I can get back to this delightful party. If you get the answer wrong, well... Let's just say, I really, really like it when men are wrong."

His hands were red with blood as they pushed against his neck.

Poor fool was too cocky and too power hungry for his own good.

Fuck I loved to watch her work. The dress was fucking made for her. It had a special corset made just to fit below all the low cuts in the back and the front. Watching her reach down the side of the fabric and grab out a shiny sharp knife? It was beautiful and had me wanting her more than I wanted my next breath of air.

"So here is the quote. There is no charm equal to tenderness of the heart."

Halle slowly bent down to where he was starting to slouch. Fuck - his eyes bugged out of his head, and I doubted it was all because of the knife or the small puncture to his neck. She was fucking toying with me.

"What is your guess? It's just so easy. Well, except I doubt you've ever had a tender heart. What would you have done to me in this room?"

She brought the knife up his cheek, but he didn't flinch. I

suppose what did it matter now? There was a gurgle of liquid, blood I supposed, as he tried to talk.

"What was that?"

She slid closer and moved the knife from his cheek to her own chest. She slid it down, a drip of blood followed. He watched her intensely, and it pissed me the fuck off.

"Do you have a guess?"

He sat down now. It was apparent the pain of his neck was too much. I'd been precise though. I left him for her but watching her here now, the glint of crazy in her eyes as she made a man pay for the sake of her own need and for the need of my family, fuck it was hot.

"Princess, be done with him or let me do my own torture."

She glared at me and took out the pink rope.

"You don't have a clue do you," she asked him and started to unwrap the rope. She turned to me.

"How slow should I make his death, babe?"

I cocked a brow. This was the second time she'd used this term. "Babe?"

She tilted her head. "Yeah. Isn't that what women call the guy they're living with?"

I took a step back and thought on this. Living with. Shit, that's what I'd done?

"You do have your own place still," was all I said.

She seemed to think on this. "Maybe. But you won't let me go to it. I assumed you just really liked me in your bed."

She bent over and started to tie the guy's ankles together, making an interesting design with the rope up to his knees. I couldn't turn my eyes from her cleavage.

My uncle's ex-friend tried to reach for her, and I tried to lunge forward, but she had a knife and cut off his finger.

"No touching old-balls-man."

God, my uncle would die if he knew what she was doing for him right now.

"Fucking call me whatever you want," I said, and moved towards her.

"Make it slow," I said, and grabbed her hips as she finished tying his legs together. I pressed the throbbing hardon she was giving me against her ass.

I groaned as she pressed her ass harder against me.

"Roll over," she said to my uncle's now very pale enemy.

He didn't listen, but she pushed him over and he fell without much help. She didn't look at me, but the next statement was directed at me.

"I need to finish tying him together. Keep your cock in your pants."

The way my uncle's ex-friend looked at her pissed me off and stoked my jealous fire. I reached around and copped a feel of her breasts. The poor fuck's eyes followed down to my hand. Once a piece of shit, always a piece of shit.

"I thought you were smart enough to know what happened when you touched my woman." He looked away and maybe tried to say something. I'd robbed him of being able to talk.

She stood up and turned in my arms.

"There, all done. He won't be going anywhere. Now what should we do?"

I didn't bother answering her before I kissed her. I didn't fucking care what we did to him, but it was going to be after I sated this need coursing through me like a god-damn freight train.

I pulled my lips away and glanced over her shoulder. "You wanted her, didn't you?"

He didn't say anything.

"You just didn't know she's beautiful and fucked in the head."

He still didn't say much of anything.

"I expected more of a fight from you. Shame. Well, if my princess can't hear you cry in pain, you can listen to her cry out in pleasure."

I thrust my fingers between her thighs, and she gasped in surprise and moaned.

"Yes, princess, let's give him a show."

I nearly came as she licked her lips and fucked me with her eyes. Her hands made quick work of my zipper and freed my ready cock.

"Fuck me, Parks. Make him hard as he bleeds out. As he watches you fuck me."

She shifted away from me until she stopped and lifted herself up on a table in the center of the room. She spread her legs wide and the thong I'd made her wear was on display and clearly wet.

"You're ready for me princess, aren't you?"

I stalked to her, gripping her knees and running my hands along the soft skin of her thighs.

"Perfect," was all I could say. I leaned over her and kissed her again as I pushed against the stupid lace. I pushed it out of the way, regretting the choice now. I was never letting her go no matter what I'd thought.

Her pelvis rose to meet the head of my cock as I pressed against her opening.

I didn't wait. I was too fucking impatient, turned on, and fucking jealous.

He'd touched her, and I didn't want her to think of anyone but me. Ever.

I thrust into her, angry and so fucking turned on. She cried out. My first thrust hit her deep inside. I fucked her fast and furious, and took her like I truly owned her. I wanted to possess her.

I slid my hand around her throat and squeezed just enough to feel her pulse as I fucked her harder and faster. I wanted to know what her pussy and her heart felt like as she fucking came for me.

She screamed and moaned and cried out my name as the walls of her core clamped down around me and I didn't stop. I kept pushing her to come again.

"Tell me, Halle. Who do you belong to?"

She could barely breathe, let alone speak, and that was exactly how I liked her.

"You. Only ever you."

I thrust into her again and let myself come inside her as her body still pulsed and pulled from me.

She collapsed against the table and fuck me, I loved watching her breasts heave with every ragged breath. I made her this way. I made her breathless.

She turned her head and looked back at the prick on the floor and seemed to find her words.

"Did you enjoy that? You know you could never make me scream like that."

Her lips slid into a twisted almost-grin as she watched him as I slid out from her and tucked myself away.

"Finish him, princess. The car will be pulling around soon."

She pulled the corset and the dress up, covering her breasts once again, and shimmied off the table.

In her hand was a knife. Pride swelled inside my chest.

She knelt down in front of him.

"It was nice meeting you. Sorry your life amounted to hurting innocent people. Enjoy hell, I hope you think of my breasts while you burn."

She reached between his legs and unzipped his pants.

"Hmm. I guess you had enough blood to get it up a little bit.

It was disappointing even when it was fully erect, I know. I had him to compare you to."

His eyes bulged, and the rasped breath he was trying to suck in through the hole in his throat got louder.

"You won't need this anymore." She cut his dick off in one quick motion and then shoved it in his mouth before she slit his throat, this time hitting the arteries and muscles and tissue underneath the skin.

"Alright babe. Wipe that table down and let's go," she said and tucked the knife back between her breasts.

I took out a handkerchief and did as she asked before wrapping her in my arms and walking away from one less problem for my family.

halle

THINGS SEEM to have changed since the Italian job. I found myself musing when I had to be alone. Something was still bothering me. Richard munched on a bug and didn't have a single care in the world. Hell, neither did I. And maybe that was the problem. Where did we stand?

There was no limit to how many bad people there were in the world. Parks was trying to be better at making sure I went with for more of his jobs.

"How's the dick?" he asked, a towel slung low on his hips.

"Richard, you ass. And he's good. He appreciates the roaches. Where did you get these again?"

He shrugged. "I imported them from a breeder. Something I didn't know even existed. Look at you, broadening my horizons."

He pulled me close and leaned his chin on my head as we both watched my little beardie. This felt strange. It almost felt like, I swallowed, like a family.

Things had been different since that first trip. Something in Parks had changed. Yes, the sex was still amazing. Yes, he was taking me out more. But when he looked at me, I couldn't understand what I was seeing.

His body was no longer just a tool for my release to help me control my crazy. No. I craved him and needed him no matter how many kills. No matter how many victims. Nothing sated my need until I topped off the night with him buried inside me. Falling asleep to him pressed against me.

What was happening?

"Parks, we need to talk."

His hand splayed over my belly, and his thumb played at my belly button. I'd failed to get dressed. What was the point when it was just him and I?

"I don't like the tone in those words, princess."

He'd taken to calling me princess or Halle, dropping rainbow almost entirely, and it was starting to feel like that's how he thought of me. As his princess or the girl that I swear had died years ago. I still couldn't explain why I'd ever given him that name. My old name.

"Look. Things are great. I love hunting with you, and you've taught me some new, amazing techniques, and you treat Richard great. But don't you think it's time I went home?"

God, how long had it been? Two, three weeks? I wasn't even sure.

"I saw your face when I said I lived with you back at that mansion. I know you didn't mean for this to be permanent. At this point do you think they forgot about me?"

I felt his chest rise and fall in a sigh.

"They don't forget anything. They think I still haven't found you."

I turned to him, loving how his hands could incite a burn of need inside me.

"What?"

I swear he almost appeared shy, boy like, as his cheeks grew pink.

"Are you blushing?"

He turned his face away and I grabbed his cheeks, forcing him back my direction.

"What is going on?"

The mint of his breath surrounded me before he spoke.

"I never told them I found you. I told them I was close, but honestly, something about you pulled to me and I didn't want to let you go just yet. I thought bringing you here would slow down their hunt when I wasn't delivering. I thought I would grow tired of you, and it would make it all easier."

My hands fell from his face as I processed what he was saying.

"But?" I asked.

"But that never happened. And now?"

I tried to pull away from him.

"Now what, you lying bastard."

He wouldn't let me go no matter how I pulled. I tried to kick his shins, and he didn't move.

"Now, I don't want to let you go."

My mouth went dry. Not let me go?

"Monsters don't get to live happily ever after," I said in a whisper.

He nodded.

"But we're not monsters. I've watched you. You have purpose, you have reason. Fuck, you make me a better killer and person."

I couldn't look at him. I couldn't see him. I didn't under-stand what he was saying.

"I... It's... I don't get to be happy," I said.

He pulled me closer, and I stopped fighting him.

"What if you did though? What if we were meant to find each other? Fate has a funny way of bringing people together."

Fate?

"I don't believe in fate. Please let me go. I need to think."

He did, and I walked off towards the bathroom, lost in my own head. It had been years since I found myself in my own head. Since I found myself lost in thought. It's what made everything easier. To not think. Not live. Not feel.

I'd missed that he was doing everything I didn't know how to live with.

He was making me feel and want and hope.

The handle of the shower pulled up without so much as a squeak. Something I'd grown used to at my little place. The water here fell like soft curtains where mine pelted away like it wasn't sure if it was spitting at me or trying to deep tissue massage.

That wasn't the only difference. My apartment was quiet and lonely.

The idea of going back to it had haunted me, but I hadn't realized why. Why I couldn't just pack up the gifts and the clothes I'd somehow acquired while being here.

I'd never worried about being caught. I'd never feared my own death. And that hadn't changed. What was bothering me?

It was that he wasn't there.

"Fuck," I said, and leaned my forehead against the tile wall of the shower stall.

"Halle?"

"Go away. You're an asshole."

I pushed myself to move and get into the warmth of the shower.

"Don't follow me." I said the words, but I didn't believe anything that I was saying.

And he didn't seem to either, because here he was, inside

the shower, pulling me into his solid muscles and running his hands over my back.

"What is it?" he asked in a voice I hardly recognized as his.

"I'm so fucking broken." It was all I could think to say. I couldn't tell him what was wrong because I barely knew anymore myself. I craved fixing everything in the world that was wrong, and it was the only thing that made me feel complete. But now? It wasn't enough, and I knew it. I knew it wasn't enough, and I didn't know what to do about it.

"It's alright. We're all a little cracked. Never broken. Not until the day you die are you broken, princess."

And for the first time in my life I debated running from my problem rather than trying to murder it.

parks

SHIT WAS GOING SIDEWAYS. I'd taken Halle on a few more jobs. Hell, I even took her to a bar and let her pick someone. But instead of growing closer, she was pulling away from me. I couldn't handle that. I wasn't overly worried about me. I would go on as I always would, except...

Fuck. I was so wrong. I'd been lying to my uncle and my family, and I didn't know why.

But I did.

She calmed the anger inside me. I hated everyone. My family used everyone and killed anyone it couldn't. Fine. I didn't really care anymore. I found it thrilling to reduce the population one psychopath at a time, but it wasn't fulfilling. No. Nothing was until I met her. She made things all seem like there was a reason. I had a purpose. It was to help her, and by helping her, I found purpose in the way and why of my life.

"Is it ready?" I said as I answered my phone.

Halle had been sitting in the chair petting that damn lizard for nearly two days. The good news is I was able to figure out the best present I could to show her everything that she was to me. I needed to keep her. She'd asked to move out too many times to count. The fact I actually viewed it as moving out was fucked up and I knew it. But that's how it felt.

No. I wouldn't allow it.

So what did one do at this point? I didn't know. It wasn't like I'd gone to a normal family function ever. But then it hit me.

I'd found Halle's past. Or a part of it. There were records that were sealed, and it kept me from digging deeper, so far. It was only a matter of time. But I was tired of waiting.

"Yes, sir. The car's downstairs and the plane is at your disposal."

I hung up and headed to the woman I couldn't seem to remember how to function without.

"Halle, princess. I have a gift for you."

Her eyes brightened, and she smiled as she turned to me.

"Another gift? You spoil me."

My heart fluttered at her words.

"You deserve the world."

Her cheeks flushed, and she looked so adorable.

"Well? Where is it?" She stood up and put the lizard away.

I followed, turning her to head to the bedroom.

"Go put on clothes. A thong and bra aren't going to work for where I'm taking you."

She peered over her shoulder and crossed her arms over her chest.

"It's a tank top, not a bra. And what kind of clothes? Like James Bond needs a whore, or it's Halle's night to pick our third wheel kind of night?"

"Ah, you have a way with words. It's a wear whatever you are comfortable in. It's a quick flight away, and the venue is casual."

She clapped her hands and skipped away. I watched her

sexy as fuck body bounce away and had to remember we needed to catch a flight not take a detour back to bed.

My phone chirped with more work from my family. Someone else to abuse and torture to get information from. Torture had lost its appeal lately, and it was all because I was worried I was losing her.

I wouldn't lose her. I couldn't lose her.

The car pulled up outside a run-down house. The damn thing looked like it was held up with duct tape and dreams. Well, fucking twisted, broken dreams from a thousand shattered minds of children.

"What are we doing here?"

I knew this could be a risk, but I also wanted to get her to see me. Me, the man who was fucking lost without her.

"I have a surprise inside."

A new side of her appeared in front of me, like the self-assured twisted-as-fuck woman I'd fallen for was now. Well, there was a haunted look on her face.

I didn't know what to think of her as she sprinted up the sidewalk. She stood still in front of the door. She didn't move. I reached forward and turned the knob, letting it swing inside. The smell was rotten, but it wouldn't matter for long.

That haunted expression on her face disappeared as the door slammed open.

God this place was gross. How had the system even allowed this? From the files, the place hadn't looked a whole lot better in its prime. I wanted to strangle whoever allowed this to happen.

The one person I could find that still remembered this shit hole said it was one of the few that would take troubled teens. It was most likely the breaking point for the troubled teens.

A shriek echoed off the other abandoned home in the nearly desolate neighborhood. Weeds for lawns, and potholes for speed bumps. The place time didn't give two fucks about was accurate.

"Halle? You okay?"

I ran in and stopped as Halle jumped up and down.

"It's Harry. How did you ever find him?"

I froze and looked around. Harry? Had I gotten the wrong guy?

"Harry? This is Martin Graves."

She stopped bouncing like a goddamn cheerleader and turned to me.

"Oh, it's the right man." Her face darkened.

"The girls and I called him Harry. Harry-ape because he had more hair on his ass than any fucking monkey we'd ever seen on TV."

She turned back to the guy she called Harry.

"Tell me, Mr. Graves. How's your junk?"

I stood back and watched her. His junk? What did she do to this guy?

"Princess? Is he why you have a strange fascination with cocks?"

My heart melted as she turned to me and smirked. "Oh, babe. You know me so well."

Back to her calling me babe, that was a great sign.

She reached into her shirt, and he knew exactly what was happening.

"Wait, Halle."

I reached for her arm.

"No. I will not wait."

I paused and pulled my hand back. "Princess, I have one more surprise. Can I give you the surprise before you kill him?"

Something new permeated the air.

"Fuck, did you just pee yourself?" I asked the guy.

The muffled words from his taped mouth sounded like," Mm-hm."

I rolled his eyes.

"Princess."

I pulled her hands into mine and this all felt right. My world was right again. I was going to get her back.

"Look around. Do you see three doors?"

She did as I asked and counted as she found each one with a spray-painted number on it.

"I don't know how to prove to you that you belong with me. I don't know how to prove to myself half the time that I deserve someone like you."

Her palms were sweaty, but I don't think it had anything to do with nerves. Probably excitement because the rapid rise and fall of her chest and the fact she couldn't seem to keep her feet still said she was antsy.

"Alright, Miss Impatient. Behind door number one, you will find a simple and yet effective bomb that will nicely burn this pond-scum and the shithole down within a few minutes."

She gasped and pulled her hands away as she practically skipped to the door with the giant spray-painted one.

"Wait, Halle. Behind door number two, are flesh-eating beetles. They're in an acrylic box connected to an even bigger, man-sized box. Should you choose this option, we will get him loaded up and you release the beetles."

She walked over to that door and looked inside. She came back and tapped her foot.

"These are an invasive species, aren't they? And what happens when he's all gone? They'll starve in that box. Oh, and not to mention if anyone comes to investigate, those babies will be put to death. Parks, we need to talk about animal cruelty."

I sighed and rubbed my face. I knew it was a bad choice when the stupid bug breeder offered them.

"Okay, okay. Bad choice. Door number three. A toy box with everything imaginable, and the room has been mostly sound proofed, although I doubt this neighborhood gives any cares at all."

She smiled and clapped her hands.

"Oh, babe. This has to be the best gift anyone has ever given me. How did you even know?"

There was no point in me standing by the door. No one would care what happened here, so I went to her side and pulled her in for a kiss.

"You forget what kind of resources I have, princess. And how motivated I can be when I want to take care of someone I love."

I swallowed. I'd said it. Fuck. I wanted to say it, but I wanted to do it after she seemed completely satisfied and happy and locked in his damn apartment in case she tried to run.

Well, I'd said it, so I might as well finish.

"Halle, I love you. I don't know when or how it all happened but stalking you has been the greatest pleasure of my life. I hope this proves to you just how much you mean to me."

She froze.

"You don't have to say anything. I just needed do this."

Was she alive? I held my fingers to her pulse and took a deep breath as each beat at least said she hadn't seized.

She looked at the guy peeing himself, yet again, and at all three doors.

"How about number 3 and 1? Help me drag him in there?"

I hesitated and then went with it. I grabbed the chair and started to pull the guy into the special toy room built just for her. She walked in and I was pretty certain even Disney World couldn't deliver this kind of awe-inspired admiration. She grabbed a large screwdriver and just as I set the chair down, she stabbed it into his hand and through to the chair.

He screamed under the tape and then passed out. She stood there looking around at everything I'd handpicked and laid out.

"What do you think? These are my favorite tools, but if anything is missing, I can have it brought out. If this takes days, you do what you need."

The guy wiggled. I guess he was awake again.

"Hmm. You know what. I'm good. Let's go set the bomb. I don't need to be here anymore."

Strange. Had I miscalculated everything?

I followed her to the front as the bang of the chair falling told me he was trying to free himself. He had mere seconds with the way she was moving, except she paused at door number two.

"Oh, hold on."

She reached in and grabbed out the bug crate the beetles were contained in.

"You're ugly little things. But that's okay. This is a judgment free zone. You do what you must to survive. I feel you beetles. I feel you." And she started to walk towards door number one.

"Parks? Be a dear and help me?"

I walked up next to her. "Anything for you." Although I still didn't know what was going through her head and it was driving me mad.

"Great. How do we—oh there? Oh, it's such a beautiful bomb. Thank you. You even labeled it with an on switch."

It was hard not to beam with pride at her gushing. But I was still fucking baffled at why she wasn't finishing the job she started in the other room. The guy was screaming, assuming I was properly interpreting the muffled sound. Oh, nope. It was screaming. He must have loosened the tape from on his lips.

"The quality of products just isn't what it used to be," I said, as she flipped the switch. The countdown started.

"Well, let's hope the quality of this guy is better. Shall we?" she said and reached for my hand.

We strolled out and kept walking.

"Behind the car princess. It's the safest distance."

She carried the box of roaches under one arm and held my hand with her other.

We knelt behind the car, staring into each other's eyes. I think that this was a good thing. I hadn't fucked this up.

We peeked over the top of the car as the ground trembled. It wasn't a very loud boom, but it was big enough that people would question if anyone had fireworks going off. Maybe. Even the fire department wouldn't be hurrying to get here.

"Halle? Before we get into the car, why didn't you make his death slower?"

She smiled at me, and I broke. She was perfect.

"Oh, simple. He hasn't had sex since he tried to rape me. And I think that is a far slower death if you ask me. He deserves to rest now."

And with that my driver grabbed the well-sealed bugs and put them in the trunk while she dragged me to the back of the car.

"So you liked my gift?"

She unzipped my pants and pulled out my cock.

"Let me just show you how much I liked it."

And the way she moved her tongue along my shaft, I wasn't sure who got a better present.

"I'M SORRY. This is one job I can't take you on. Everyone will be there."

I punched him as hard as I could.

"This isn't fair. When do I get to meet them? You can't hide me forever. It's going to be awkward at Emilee's wedding."

He stopped buttoning up his shirt and looked at me.

"Emilee's wedding? How do you know about that?"

I shrugged and pulled out the invitation from the chair that I'd claimed as my sadness spot.

"I'm burning that damn chair when I get back," he threatened.

I glared and walked over to him. He was leaving me, something he hadn't done since he gave me my gift. The perfect gift. The strange fear in his eyes had gone away, although I still hadn't said I love you. Not yet. And he didn't seem to care. He hadn't pushed me. Or maybe he had.

He'd become insatiable. I wasn't sure even I could keep up with this pace. It was like every day that I left the words unsaid, he had to reassure himself I was still here.

And why hadn't I said the words? I didn't know. But something inside me was certain it had a lot to do with, yes, he loved me, but here I was, still hidden.

"Maybe I saw this on the tray of food the other day. You were in the shower when they brought it up and the beautiful writing. Well, it was obvious."

He ran his hands through his hair, and he swore under his breath.

"You know you can't go, right?"

That was exactly the wrong answer.

"Fuck you. Fuck your perfect fucking gift. Fuck you and this fucking apartment. Just fuck you."

He tried to grab a hold of me and pull me into him, but I was done. I didn't think I could be hurt but this hurt.

"You don't get to hide me like some fucking slave. I am a person and I have needs."

He followed me as I ranted through the apartment.

"Halle, princess. Stop. I know. I take you out. If I had friends, you'd know them. I just haven't figured out how to handle my uncle. You have to understand that if I don't kill you, then he will find someone to do it."

I grabbed something hard and expensive, some stupid vase that had been here before me, and I threw it.

"Then let's go, kill me, you idiot. Like, do they even know what I look like?"

He paused.

"For someone who looks so damn smart in a suit and has all these fancy degrees and shit, you sure don't seem to know much. What did you tell them? We can find someone, toss her in my apartment and burn it to the ground."

He finished buttoning his shirt, and then, with a set look on his face, approached me. Or maybe charged me. His lips were on mine, and he was kissing me like my life depended on it.

"Alright, princess. You're too fucking smart for me.

Tomorrow we'll find someone who will pass as you. But tonight? Stay home. Things have hit a new level of fucked and my family is on a rampage."

He let my feet touch the ground and he kissed me one more time.

"It will be a late night, but I promise I will be back. I got you that ice cream you like so much, and dick has a few silkworms, special delivery. There's a new forensics show all queued up for you too."

It was really hard to stay mad at him when he was being so sweet.

"You promise tomorrow we can go kill a few people? One that looks just like me?"

He smiled.

"Yes. Promise. One that looks just like you. Use my laptop and scour the police database while I'm gone."

The world felt like it had just been lifted off my shoulders. Like this was the last barrier holding us apart. My past was always a little in the way of me, but the nightmares seemed to be better with him holding me. I just needed this. To know that I could have something normal and real.

"Okay. I'll pick her out tonight then and be ready to go tomorrow night. Can we do matching outfits too?"

He rolled his eyes, and I could tell he was about to give in when his phone beeped again.

"Halle, whatever you want. I gotta go. The boys are downstairs. I love you. Stay home until we get this sorted."

I nodded as he grabbed his jacket.

"Oh, wait." I ran up to him and climbed him like a monkey. "I have a gift for you."

He gave me a funny look, or rather a look that wasn't something I think the world would ever see.

"So I've been trying to figure out what to get the guy who

has everything. Which is really hard when I can't leave to go shopping. So, look what I found."

I pulled out my Monday panties.

"It's so romantic that you kept them."

Yes, this was the venerable face that only I got to see. I folded up the panties.

"In memory of our very first meet up, take these with you tonight so I'm there in spirit."

I tucked them into his lapel pocket and gave him a peck on the cheek.

And that was the moment I decided was a good time to return the words he wanted. Why? Because, at the end of the day, I think that this was love. Or the closest to love that either of us could give each other.

"I love you, Parks. Now go, so I can masturbate at the memory of you."

He winked at me and put me down, kissing my forehead as he did.

"I love you, my twisted princess."

I did what Parks asked. I fed Richard one silkworm and enjoyed him devouring the thing like it was his own personal mission. He was a lizard after my own heart.

I tossed on a pair of PJs that Parks bought for me. Everything was something he bought for me. These were at least cotton, but still sheer and comfy. He liked me in simple more than he liked me in fancy. He liked me for me.

"Alright, Richard. Ice cream for me, and then let's see if we can guess the cause of death from the blood patterns."

I padded to the kitchen, grabbing out a spoon when the elevator dinged.

"Parks, you forget something?"

I had just turned around when something sharp bit into my neck.

"What the hell? That's not very nice, you asshat." The room blurred and then came back into focus, but my arms were heavy.

I tried to swing myself around and least hit someone with the useless things, but then my legs wobbled, and I started to go down.

"Parks is going to be pissed."

I could watch everything going on. I got to stare at the nasty ass of the guy that tossed me over his shoulder. I got to watch them as they tried to get me into the trunk of the SUV and they banged my damn head twice. Once I could talk, they were getting yelled at.

I couldn't see much else for a bit. The drive was short and closer to the end there were trees to watch pass by. Joy. Trees.

The engine cutoff and the doors opened.

"Fuck. She's hot. What a waste of a good pussy," said one of the guys. Maybe he looked a little like Parks. Hard to tell from one eye.

Another guy came around.

"Well, she should have thought about that before she killed a Rossi."

Good Lord. "Me having a hot pussy would have affected killing a Rossi?" I said. I tried to smile and got a little movement. Sweet, things were coming back.

"Shit. The stuffs wearing off. Get her inside and tied down," said another.

"What is this the four stooges? Is anyone here of legal drinking age?" I chided as they manhandled me over a shoulder again.

My arms hung limp. Annoying.

"Shut up. Just shut the fuck up."

I ignored him and started to laugh. I couldn't do anything physically, but I was amazing at psychological warfare.

"Stop laughing bitch."

"Why would I?"

The guy started to growl. But it was sort of the opposite of scary.

I laughed harder.

"Shut up."

I laughed harder.

They got me inside and plopped me onto a chair, where they proceeded to tie me up.

"Make sure you get my torso, I'm really having a hard time sitting up straight."

My head lolled to the side to prove my point.

"How did Parks live with her for so long? Twenty minutes and I'm done with her."

I laughed again.

"Why are you laughing?"

There was no point in asking names. I just didn't care. They wouldn't matter soon.

"But I have the best secret ever. You're in so much trouble."

Dude just glared at me.

"Best secret? Fuck me. Why do I feel like anything you say is going to have me regretting my choice?" asked one of them.

I shrugged. "Men are rarely confident in their choices. Anything that emasculates you makes you feel regret."

He walked forward and slapped me. The taste of blood on my lip made me stop laughing simply to lap it up.

"Mmm. Delicious. So now do you want to know my secret?"

He backed away.

"Fine. I'll tell you, anyway."

My hands felt a bit less numb, this was nothing that I wouldn't survive from.

"These zip ties are awful tight. How do you expect me to cut off your cock, assuming I can find it, if my hands are numb?"

He didn't seem to know if he wanted to come closer or stay away. He seemed to just keep pacing.

"Just shut up. I can't kill you until, well I can't kill you yet. So just shut up."

I wiggled my hands again deciding what was the best way to proceed. I would break this asshole first. That was certain.

"Okay. Well, since you won't ask. You are in so much trouble because of my boyfriend. You think I have issues? Have you met Parks?"

This got his attention. He circled me.

"It's not polite to attack people from the back," I heckled.

"Your boyfriend? Your boyfriend? Parks Rossi? He doesn't have girlfriends. He fucks them and leaves them shattered and broken. He did it to my sister."

I bristled. Sister?

"I'm not dumb enough to think he was a monk before me, so fine. He fucked your sister. Sorry. Don't care. He's mine now and he loves me."

I could feel the hot breath of him against my neck. I didn't like this. I never had. I never enjoyed being touched. Until Parks. Everything about him was different. Everything about me with him was different and there was no going back. I would try and escape, but maybe I could wait a little while. Wait for him to come for me. Choices, choices.

I shivered and wiggled my head at the next hot breath.

"Personal space much?" I asked.

I could feel his greedy fingers pushing aside my hair. Or the hair that had fallen from my ponytail.

"He's supposed to marry my sister, but he's had a few secrets. Well guess what? Times up."

I wiggled what I could. Feeling was starting to come back. A few more minutes of babbling and small talk and then I could work my way through getting out. I had a knife strapped around my upper thigh and somehow these idiots hadn't seen it yet. Except his next words stole my breath.

"Who do you think sold you out?"

I turned to him and smirked, turning on the switch before Parks.

"Well, good news then. You can't sellout the crazy chick. Now how do you want your death to be?"

parks

"WHAT THE FUCK is going on here?"

My uncle stopped in front of a family I hated. A family that I'd broken ties with when my cousin died. Thank the fucking Lord.

"Parks, my boy. It's wonderful to see you," said Mark Voigt.

Fuck. What was going on here? I stepped back only to be stopped by two bodies, both of which reported to me.

"What the hell. Let me out of here."

They shifted, and one whispered. "Sorry, boss. We were told we'd be sleeping with the fish if we let you go."

"Parks, my boy. We have a little deal to fix up here. You remember Cara, Mark's oldest and heiress to Voigt industries? When Cyrus was killed, the engagement was broken between our two families but in recent weeks it's come to light that Cara here knows who you are. She specifically asked for the contract to be transferred to you."

Fuck me running.

"I can't. Sorry. I'm already spoken for."

Cara's face wrinkled into something ugly.

"Ah, yes. Come over here son."

Son? Fuck this wasn't good.

My uncle came up to me and pulled me a few feet away from the circle of assholes. The field was lit by headlights from several vehicles from all sides.

"She's been taken care of. I'm not sure what you are playing at, but the woman in your apartment looked an awful lot like Cyrus's killer. The one you were tracking down."

My knuckles cracked with the force of my fists clenching.

"Looked? What do you mean looked? She is mine. Not yours, or Cyrus's killer. I promise you a body tomorrow."

He laughed, and I hated the sound. I hated the way his gray hair seemed to defy the wind blowing through this fucking field.

"Son, by the time we get back to town she will be dead. Voigt's men have her and Lucas. Unless you agree to this marriage. You fucked up and didn't keep the heir from fucking his life up. You should have been my son. Looks like it's a win-win for me."

Inside I was screaming.

"You don't fucking kill my woman if I marry Cara? What kind of fucking win is that?"

He smiled and there was the Rossi crazy. The one that I grew up knowing. The one that shaped who I was and who I had to become to survive. The one that got my father killed. None of us were sane.

I looked around at the group behind me. Options. I needed options. Maybe I needed time.

My phone buzzed. The elevator had been activated, and no one had been authorized up there. I'd made sure of that tonight. I'd thought tonight was something very different.

"Win-win for me, son. Parks, have I not been good to you? Given you unlimited access to anyone and everything in this empire? You owe me."

This time I did scream.

"Owe you? Owe you? For what? If anything, you owe me."

The phone rang and my uncle, James Rossi, answered in all his kingly ways.

"Kill her," was all he said, and I lost my shit.

Coming soon! Part 2
Touch Her and Die!

Chelle grew up in a home that snarky was the only way of survival. Did she get therapy growing up? No. So what did she turn to? Books. And in those books she realized you could let your freak flag fly.

So here she is with a lizard, two dogs, some kids, and a husband writing snarky dark romance instead of seeking out the help she probably needs.

Enjoy the ride.

Website: https://www.chellewolfe.com/

Newsletter: https://www.subscribepage.com/chellewolfe

facebook.com/ChelleWolfeAuthor

tiktok.com/chellewolfeauthor

instagram.com/chellewolfeauthor

bookbub.com/authors/chelle-wolfe